"I h

Nathan ran a hand across his forehead.

"What are you protecting him from? If I *am* Kyle's mother, I'm going to want to spend more time with him. I want him to know who I am. How will you handle that? Will you try to shut me out of his life or include me in it?"

The more he studied Sara's features, the more Nathan saw Kyle's. "I don't have the answer, Sara, not now, not yet. There's no point jumping ahead of ourselves."

"I'd like to know where my life is going and what I can expect next."

He recognized that desire. "There's no way to plan for the unexpected and you know it."

He saw the uncertainty of the situation was shaking her world. There was nothing he could do about that.

He just hoped it didn't shake his, too.

Dear Reader,

When I develop a hero, I create the type of man I would choose as a life partner. My three heroes in this series—the Barclay brothers—have many qualities in common. They feel deeply, although they don't always show it. They will not hesitate to go out of their way to protect the people they love. They long to be fathers so they can share their view of the world as well as the love their family has given them.

But Nathan, Sam and Ben Barclay also have individual personalities. Once a financial analyst, now an innkeeper, Nathan takes life and fatherhood seriously. A veterinarian, Sam loves animals as well as kids and uses his sense of humor to make a point. Ben, a district attorney, although cynical at times, wants good to prevail.

Which hero do you prefer? After you read the series, I'd like to know.

Readers can e-mail me through my Web site at www.karenrosesmith.com or write to me at P.O. Box 1545, Hanover, PA 17331.

I hope you enjoy reading my *Dads in Progress* miniseries as much as I enjoyed writing it.

All my best,

Karen Rose Smith

THE DADDY DILEMMA

KAREN ROSE SMITH

SPECIAL EDITION®

Published by Silhouette Books

America's Publisher of Contemporary Romance

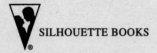

SILHOUETTE BOOKS

ISBN-13: 978-0-373-24884-1
ISBN-10:   0-373-24884-9

THE DADDY DILEMMA

Copyright © 2008 by Karen Rose Smith

Visit Silhouette Books at www.eHarlequin.com

Printed in U.S.A.

Books by Karen Rose Smith

Silhouette Special Edition

Abigail and Mistletoe #930
The Sheriff's Proposal #1074
His Little Girl's Laughter #1426
Expecting the CEO's Baby #1535
Their Baby Bond #1588
Take a Chance on Me #1599
Which Child Is Mine? #1655
*Cabin Fever #1682
Custody for Two #1753
The Baby Trail #1767
Expecting His Brother's Baby #1779
†The Super Mom #1797
††Falling for the Texas Tycoon #1807
The Daddy Dilemma #1884

Silhouette Books

The Fortunes of Texas
Marry in Haste...

Logan's Legacy
A Precious Gift

The Fortunes of Texas: Reunion
The Good Doctor

Signature Select

Secret Admirer
"Dream Marriage"

"Promoted to Mom"

*Montana Mavericks: Gold Rush Grooms
†Talk of the Neighborhood
††Logan's Legacy Revisited

KAREN ROSE SMITH

Award-winning and bestselling author Karen Rose Smith has seen sixty novels published since 1991. Living in Pennsylvania with her husband—who was her college sweetheart—and their two cats, she has been writing full-time since the start of her career. Lately, in addition to writing, she has been crafting jewelry with her husband. She finds designing necklaces and bracelets relaxing enough to let her mind weave plots while she's beading! Readers can receive updates on Karen's latest releases and write to her through her Web site at www.karenrosesmith.com or at P.O. Box 1545, Hanover, PA 17331.

To my aunt Rose Marie who has made
Minnesota her home. Love, Karen.

Prologue

She was going to save her mother's life.

As Sara Hobart lay on the surgical center gurney, she knew she'd done the right thing. She'd had no choice.

Her friend Joanne, who worked at the fertility clinic, sat by her bed, her black ringlets tumbling around her face as she declared vehemently, "No one should be denied treatment because they can't afford to pay. With the ten thousand for donating your eggs, you'll have enough to give the hospital to go through with your mother's transplant. Right?"

"Along with the fund-raising money, we'll have enough. We can tell her doctor to begin treatment. Thank you so much for helping me. For being here today. I never thought

I'd do anything like this—" Emotion tightened Sara's throat. Her mom deserved every chance to prolong her life, and Sara would do anything in her power to make it happen.

Joanne patted Sara's hand. "You're not only helping your mom, you're giving a childless couple a chance to conceive. Your eggs are going to a worthy recipient."

Of course her friend couldn't divulge the names of the people she'd be helping. The couple's criteria had been simple: eggs from a healthy woman, twenty-eight or younger, with a 1300+ SAT score. A law student, Sara had fit the bill. When Joanne had given her the idea, it had been a godsend.

"The couple you're donating to already had two in vitro attempts that failed," Joanne further explained.

Sara never would have considered going through this procedure if her mother hadn't gotten ill. But bone marrow transplant treatment was considered experimental with her mom's rare blood disorder, and was more expensive than they had ever realized. Although Sara had written appeal letter after appeal letter, the insurance company had denied coverage. Because her mother didn't have time to wait any longer, Sara had decided the only thing to do was to raise the money herself. Joanne as well as other friends had helped with the fund-raisers in their small town ten miles outside of Minneapolis, but they'd come up thousands short, even for the down payment.

When Sara had been accepted as a donor by the clinic, she'd told her mom, and they'd both cried tears of relief…and of hope. Sara couldn't imagine a world without her mother in it. She'd never had a father, never had uncles or aunts or cousins. She and her mom only had each other, and were best friends. But Joanne was a very good friend, too. In fact, she was taking the afternoon off to drive her to her apartment.

Sara pushed her blond hair from her temple, ready to take the next step to make her mom well. "When I get home, I can make the call to the financial services director at Saint Bartholomew's Hospital. Mom can start treatment as soon as they can fit her in."

Although Sarah was hopeful, fear still gripped her...the same fear that had gnawed at her ever since her mother received her diagnosis. Would the transplant work?

Underneath worry for her mom, Sara thought about the procedure she'd just experienced. She had lots of eggs. Giving away a few wouldn't affect her life at all. In spite of her career, she *did* want children some day. After she became a partner in a law firm, she would consider it.

Some day.

Would her mother see someday with her?

Sarah could only pray she would.

Chapter One

Six Years Later

Sara opened the heavy oak door into Pine Grove Lodge, anxiety tightening her chest, her heart pounding hard. She wasn't sure she should be here, but she had to find out if Nathan Barclay's son was *her* son. He might not be. Her eggs might not have been instrumental in giving the Barclays a child. But the dates lined up—her donation and Kyle's birth. She *had* to know for sure. Her accident and hysterectomy in June had devastated her…until during her recuperation, Joanne, who'd left the fertility clinic a few years ago to take a more lucrative position elsewhere, had revealed Nathan Barclay's name.

Moving into the great room, Sara found no one standing at the long mahogany counter.

A door opened at the rear of the room and a tall, broad-shouldered man carrying an armful of logs came in and kicked the door shut with one booted foot. As he passed the floor-to-ceiling stone fireplace and caught sight of her, he smiled. But it was a forced smile that didn't light up his eyes, which were the same color as the gray November sky outside.

Sara recognized Nathan Barclay from the photograph she'd found in an article about him and his dad restoring this resort in their hometown of Rapid Creek, Minnesota. Still reeling from her mom's death from cancer a year ago, as well as the accident that had taken away Sara's ability to have children, she'd looked him up on the Internet, and she'd found more than she'd ever imagined. Most important, she'd learned he was a widower and had a son who was five.

She hadn't made an impulsive decision that could affect several lives. After her recuperation, she'd returned to her law firm, working seventy to eighty hours a week. But after two months, she'd decided to use vacation time, and had packed a suitcase, grabbed her laptop and headed to the Wisconsin Dells to think. Two days into her getaway, she'd found herself driving to Rapid Creek, searching for answers.

Now here she was, practically shaking in her sneakers.

"If you're looking for a room, I'm sorry, but we don't have any vacancies. This time of year we're usually full." Nathan Barclay's deep voice resonated through Sara, making her anxiety grab a stronger hold.

Straightening her shoulders and taking a breath, she waited only a heartbeat before replying, "I'm not looking for a room."

At her words his dark brows quirked up. Turning away from her, he lowered the armful of logs onto the hearth. Her heart pounded so hard she thought it would burst from her chest.

Finally, he brushed off his hands and crossed to her. Only two feet away, she noticed strands of gray at the temples of his dark brown hair, lines above his brows and around his eyes and mouth.

"If you don't need a room for the night, how can I help you?" he asked, looking puzzled.

"Mr. Barclay, I'm Sara Hobart."

He showed no recognition of her name.

State the facts. Make him understand.

"Almost six years ago, on January 23, I donated eggs at the Brighton Fertility Clinic in Minneapolis. I found out your wife benefited from that donation. I'm wondering... I believe..."

His firm jaw set. His stance became defensive.

Forgetting her training as a lawyer, and too personally involved to weigh her words, she plunged in and asked, "Did your wife conceive from that in vitro procedure?"

The man before her was on his guard. His eyes were dark with stormy outrage. "How could you *possibly* have gotten my name? That information is confidential."

"Mr. Barclay, I don't mean you or Kyle any harm—"

"How do you know my son's name?" Barclay's voice

was rough and he was looking at her as if he should call the police.

More determined than ever to find out if she was Kyle's mother, if she had a legitimate claim, she stretched out her hand in a pleading gesture. "I'm a lawyer. I have easy access to databases. If you'd let me start at the beginning—"

"I don't want you to start anywhere. I want you to leave. If it's true you donated eggs at Brighton, then you also signed a release form relinquishing any rights. So if you think I'm going to pay you another cent, you're sadly mistaken."

She shook her head. "I don't want money. I…I was in an automobile accident and had to have a hysterectomy. I looked you up on the Internet and found out you're a widower. When I searched public records, I discovered your wife died in childbirth and so did Kyle's twin brother."

"You had no right to invade my privacy!"

"I can't have children, Mr. Barclay. I'd like to meet Kyle. That's all." Her voice shook on the last word.

After a long, silent pause and a penetrating search of her eyes, he said firmly, "I'm not going to let a stranger just waltz into our home."

Trying to keep her composure, reminding herself calm reason could possibly make a dent in Nathan Barclay's armor, she took a folded sheet of paper from her coat pocket and handed it to him. "Here are my credentials and a brief background. I've also provided references. My friends and neighbors don't know why I'm here, but they can tell you anything you need to know about me."

He took the sheet of paper and glanced at it, then asked in a low voice, "What do you *really* want?"

"I want to meet Kyle. Afterward, I'll return to Minneapolis."

"Just like that?"

"Just like that. I give you my word. I know I have no rights here. I just want to meet him." Because if she did, she'd know, wouldn't she? Wouldn't instinct tell her if Kyle was hers?

His gaze raked over her shoulder-length blond hair, her jeans, sneakers and rose, cable-knit sweater under her suede jacket. She knew he was trying to assess whether or not she was a danger to him. But his gaze passing over her made her feel self-conscious and…warm.

"Miss Hobart, your word means nothing to me. You said you're a lawyer. If you are, you know the document you signed was valid."

Yes, it was. She didn't need a custody lawyer to tell her that. She motioned to the paper she'd given him. "I've written the name of the bed-and-breakfast where I'm staying on the back of my references. I'll be there until Friday."

Silence echoed from floor to ceiling in the large room. Finally, he asked, "And after Friday?"

"I'll be returning to Minneapolis." When his stone-cold expression gave away none of his thoughts, she added, "Please put yourself in my shoes, Mr. Barclay. Since my accident, my life has been in turmoil. Actually, it's come to a standstill. I need to meet Kyle to move on."

After he folded the sheet of paper she'd given him, he shoved it into the pocket of his Western-cut shirt. "I think you should go."

Sara could see that nothing else she said would move him or change his mind. After a last look into his eyes, dark gray now with the turbulence she'd obviously caused, she gave a slight nod and retraced her steps to the front door. As she left Pine Grove Lodge, she hoped Nathan Barclay would try to put himself in her shoes and call her before Friday.

If he didn't, she might never meet Kyle and learn whether or not he was her son.

"What did Ben say?" Galen Barclay looked worried as Nathan hung up the phone.

"I have to check on Kyle." Nathan was still reeling from his encounter with Sara Hobart that afternoon. Calling his brother Ben, who was an assistant district attorney in Albuquerque, had seemed to be a good idea. But Ben's experience with women had left his brother cynical.

"Kyle will be fine for a few minutes," his father insisted. "He's playing with his fire trucks in his room."

Ever since his son had been born early, at twenty-six weeks, Nathan had been protective of him. When he'd developed asthma, Nathan hadn't wanted him out of his sight. At his father's urging he'd relaxed a bit with all of his coddling, but he still kept a close eye on Kyle.

"So what was Ben's advice?" his dad asked again.

"He told me not to worry. He assured me that if Sara Hobart signed a release form when she donated her eggs— he believes the word *donated* doesn't apply, since she received $10,000 in exchange for them—she doesn't have a parental leg to stand on. He thinks she's simply a gold digger, and I tend to agree." Though that's what Nathan's head told him, he remembered the pain in the woman's eyes when she'd spoken of having a hysterectomy.

"You said *she's* a lawyer."

"Yes. I called one of her references, a neighbor. I also checked the roster of attorneys at the firm listed on her credentials. Apparently she *is* a lawyer in Charles Frank's firm. When I searched the Internet, there was an account of her accident this summer. A man in his forties who'd taken cold medication fell asleep while he was driving, crossed the highway and hit her head on. From the sound of it, she's lucky she wasn't killed. Everything she told me seems to be true."

After a reflective silence, his dad commented, "If she's a lawyer in Charles Frank's law firm—it's the biggest and best in Minneapolis—I doubt she's looking for a handout. You know Ben. He believes women are out for whatever they can get. This Hobart woman could be on the level. What if she *is* the one who enabled you and Colleen to have a child? What if she *is* Kyle's mother?"

Nathan's heart rejected that idea instantaneously. *Colleen* was Kyle's mother. Nathan had pictures of his deceased wife all over the house. He wanted Kyle to know her in some small way. *He* knew what it was like to grow up without a mother. His own had left him and his two brothers to pursue her career and live a life better than the one she'd found in Rapid Creek. She hadn't looked back. Unlike his own attempt to give Kyle a sense of Colleen, his dad had tried to wipe *his* wife's memory from all of their lives. After she'd left, Galen had never spoken of her again. Not until Nathan had asked questions when he'd graduated from high school.

"Son, Colleen is gone." His dad was always blunt when he wanted to make a point. "She isn't here to put her arms around Kyle when he needs a hug. He can't hear her voice in the middle of the night when he's scared."

Nathan's anger rose quickly, the same anger that had shaken its fist at fate when that force had taken Colleen and Kyle's twin, Mark, away from him. "*I* give him hugs. *I* sit with him when he has bad dreams."

"But are you enough? Am I enough? Is Val enough? None of us can take the place of a mother."

Nathan and Galen both depended on Val Lindstrom, the housekeeper Nathan had hired to look after Kyle when he was busy at the lodge or guiding tourists who stayed there. "Ben, Sam and I grew up just fine with only you to take care of us," Nathan said.

"Maybe you did and maybe you didn't. I don't think Ben will ever trust a woman enough to settle down with her. And that stems back to your mother deserting us. And Sam... Maybe he chose poorly because I never taught him how to choose wisely."

Since his dad rarely brought up the subject of their

mother's desertion, Nathan decided to take advantage of this opportunity. "Why didn't you ever remarry?"

"Because not many women could take on three boys and like it. I never met anyone willing to try." Galen picked up the paper on the counter that Sara Hobart had given to Nathan. "What harm would come from inviting this Hobart woman to meet Kyle? I'm sure he gets tired of just seeing you, me and Val."

"What harm?" Nathan couldn't believe his dad wouldn't acknowledge the obvious. "If she sees him, she might want to spend more time with him. What if she stays in Rapid Creek?"

Waving that idea away with a flick of his hand, Galen responded, "She has a first-class job in Minneapolis. She didn't go to school all those years just to give it up."

Something else troubled Nathan even more. "What if Kyle likes her?"

"And what if he doesn't?" his dad protested. "What if they don't get along at all? What if his asthma scares her?"

Even if he entertained that possibility, Nathan was unsettled by the idea of inviting Sara Hobart into his home. "I think we'd be taking a big gamble letting her meet him."

"Aren't you taking a bigger gamble never telling Kyle the truth?"

"He's not old enough to understand."

Galen's eyes were a steady gray, showing the wisdom of his sixty-four years. "When will he *be* old enough? When he's twelve? When he's sixteen?"

"Dad—"

"You can't ignore the truth, even though you've tried. You've convinced yourself you and Colleen were the only two people involved."

Yes, he had. Ever since Colleen had been implanted with the embryos, they'd dismissed the donor. She'd been a means for Colleen to get pregnant, and that was all.

But now that donor had a face—a very pretty face...and green eyes identical to Kyle's. "I'm not sure we should let her into our lives."

"She's already in your life if she's Kyle's mother."

That was a very big *if.*

Sara Hobart had given her word she'd go back to Minneapolis after she met Kyle. Could Nathan believe her?

When Sara stepped into Nathan Barclay's log home, she felt like an interloper. But it didn't matter how she felt. Only meeting Kyle mattered.

Nathan stood in the living room amid comfortable green-and-brown-plaid corduroy furniture. His jaw was set in an uncompromising line, as if he was sorry he'd invited her here.

As her gaze locked with his, a tingle of awareness ran through her. She ignored it. "I was grateful you called. I honestly thought you wouldn't. What changed your mind?"

"You checked me out. I checked on you. Everything you told me was true."

"You didn't expect it to be?"

He shook his head. "There are lots of crazy people in the world, Miss Hobart."

"It's Sara." For some reason she believed that if he used her given name, there would at least be a tenuous thread of communication between them.

He didn't use her name and his tone was severe. "Before I call Kyle from his room, there's something you need to know. He has asthma."

Instantly concerned, Sara asked, "Is it serious? I don't know much about the condition."

"It can be life threatening." As she absorbed that, he went on. "I'm not being dramatic. When he had his first attack, he was three. I'd painted two of the bedrooms in the lodge and had him there with me. He started having trouble breathing, then he began to wheeze. I didn't know what was happening, but thank goodness I brought him downstairs while Dad called emergency services."

Although Nathan's face was stoic, Sara could imagine the fear and panic that must have shaken him. "Is Kyle on medication?"

"Yes. And he uses inhalers."

"Are there particular things that cause an attack?" She should know what they were. A little voice asked, *Why, if this is the only time you're going to see Kyle?* She pushed that question away.

"Strong smells like cleaning solutions or scented candles. Extreme cold. Too much dust." Nathan took a few steps closer. "And emotional upset. I don't want him upset. I told him a friend was coming to visit, that's all."

She had to look up a good six inches to meet Nathan's eyes. They were almost threatening, and the message was clear. If she did anything to upset Kyle, he'd toss her out.

Still, amazingly, she didn't feel intimidated, because she understood. As a parent, she'd want to protect her child that fiercely, too. "I understand."

The November weather was becoming colder. She'd worn jeans and a sweater again, topped by her suede jacket. She unbuttoned it, hoping Kyle's dad would let her stay more than five minutes.

As she slid out of one sleeve, Nathan was beside her. "I'll hang this in the closet."

Relieved, she smiled at him and motioned to a bakery bag she'd set on the arm of the sofa with her purse. "I brought chocolate chip cookies. Does Kyle have any dietary restrictions?"

"No. No food allergies, thank goodness. And he does love chocolate. It was thoughtful of you to bring them."

Nathan was acting superbly polite. She wished he'd just be himself and say what he was thinking. "It's not a bribe," she assured him. "Chocolate and little boys just seem to go together."

When he ·didn't respond, she tried again. "You told Kyle I was a friend. He'll know that's not true if he senses your hostility."

"I'm not hostile."

She wasn't going to argue with him. "Can we pretend to be friendly for Kyle's sake?"

Nathan blew out a long sigh. "Look, Miss—"

"Sara," she reminded him.

"All right. Sara. I'm not pleased about you being here. I just want this over with. I'm not going to pretend otherwise."

"Kyle will pick up whatever you feel."

"Maybe. On the other hand, if I'm not feeling anything, he won't pick up anything. While you spend time with him, I'll be in the kitchen."

"You're going to let me sink or swim on my own?" She meant the comment to lighten the tension a bit. But it didn't, and she murmured, "You're hoping I sink." So much for being friends. "Okay, Mr. Barclay. How much time are you going to give me?"

"Let's just see how it goes."

She supposed that meant if she and Kyle got along well, he'd give her a little more time. But whether that was fifteen minutes or an hour, she knew he wouldn't say. She was a planner, an organizer. But today she was going to have to go with the flow whether she liked it or not.

However, going with the flow required a certain amount of trust. She didn't have much trust anymore—certainly not in men. In her experience men walked away when life didn't go the way they planned.

How she wished her mother was still alive. She could give her guidance. But her mom was gone and Sara had no family. "Can I meet Kyle now?"

Carrying her jacket to the closet just inside the door, Nathan hung it up. Then, after a long look at her, he called, "Kyle. Come on out here a minute, will you? There's someone I want you to meet."

Sara's heart raced so fast she couldn't count the beats.

When the five-year-old appeared, tears brimmed in her eyes and she quickly blinked them away. She couldn't be overcome by emotion. A child wouldn't understand that, and she didn't want to scare him. She just wanted to talk with him and *be* with him.

She didn't need a DNA test to know right away that he was her son. She could see the evidence in his green eyes, so like hers…and in the tilt of his smile, so like her mother's.

As he ran up to his dad and stood expectantly waiting for an introduction, while glancing surreptitiously at her, she noted he had Nathan's dark brown hair and a very defined little chin. He'd probably be as stubborn as his father someday.

"Sara," Nathan said, as if he'd been using her first name for years, "this is my son, Kyle. Kyle, this is that friend I told you about. Her name is Sara."

Not knowing exactly how to proceed, she approached him slowly. "Hi there, Kyle."

As a lawyer, Sara negotiated and dealt with adults on a daily basis. She suspected kids didn't like to be crowded any more than grown-ups, so she kept some distance between them.

Motioning to the two fire trucks she'd spotted by the bookshelves, she decided to jump in with both feet. After all, her time here could be extremely limited. "I noticed your aerial truck and pumper. Were you rescuing people from those tall buildings?" She'd taken a guess that the bookshelves were high-rises.

Kyle, who was almost standing behind his dad's hip, took a step closer to her. "Those are apartment buildings," he said with some excitement. "How did you know?"

Sara crouched down to his level and looked him straight in the eye. "When I was a little girl, I had a nurse doll. I used our television stand as the hospital. Each shelf was a different floor."

Grinning widely now, Kyle let go of his dad's pant leg and stood even closer. "Do you want to play with me? We could rescue everybody and put the fire out."

Before she said yes, she glanced at Nathan. He was the one making decisions, and she couldn't take a wrong step.

He gave a tight nod.

She wished she could take Kyle into her arms and give him a hug, but she knew it was too soon for that. Also, if she did, she had a feeling Nathan might panic and pull Kyle away.

Instead, she said calmly, "I'd love to play with you."

Kyle ran to the bookshelves and dropped down onto the floor, cross-legged. "You can drive the pumper truck. I like to drive the aerial. But I'll let you climb up, too."

In spite of herself, she laughed. "That's good…because I don't think I can get to the top shelf without using the ladder."

Like any five-year-old involved in his own world, Kyle didn't ask who she was, where she was from or why she was there. All he cared about was the fact she was playing with him.

They'd been rescuing pretend inhabitants in the book-shelf apartments for about a half hour when Nathan called from the kitchen. "Time for milk and cookies. Come in here to eat them, though. I wouldn't want the crumbs to clog up your fire hoses."

Apparently the man had a sense of humor when he interacted with his son, Sara thought.

Kyle called back, "In a minute, Dad."

Suddenly Nathan appeared, only a few feet away. "I'll set the timer." He winked at Sara. "His minutes can get awfully long sometimes."

Gazing up at Nathan—noticing again his muscular body; his angular face, which was interesting rather than purely handsome; the slight smile that was all for his son—Sara felt a tummy-twirling sensation. When she considered the situation, her joy at simply being here with Kyle, she dismissed it as excitement. However, when she was sitting in the rustic kitchen with its hurricane lamp chandelier above the round pine table, Nathan looming like a guardian angel between her and Kyle, she wasn't so sure. Although all of her attention was focused on the five-year-old, when she reached for a napkin in the center of the table and Nathan did so at the same time, their fingers brushed and heat zipped up her arm.

He jerked away and so did she. But the sensation remained.

A little later, when she leaned forward to ask Kyle his favorite flavor of ice cream, her leg grazed Nathan's. She shifted away, but apparently not soon enough. Warmth spread through her body so rapidly she thought the temperature in the house had gone up ten degrees.

Knowing Nathan would soon cut off her time with Kyle, she finished her cookie and wiped her fingers on her napkin. "Are you in kindergarten this year?"

Crumbs on his upper lip, Kyle shook his head. "Nope. Dad says next year will be soon enough. I'm gonna be homeschooled."

She looked to Nathan for an explanation.

"I thought I'd hire a tutor. With Kyle's asthma it might be best to keep him at home."

"Just for kindergarten?"

Nathan shrugged. "We'll see how it goes."

She couldn't keep the words from escaping. "Interaction with other kids is important."

"So is his health."

Biting her tongue, Sara reached for her glass of milk. She had no say in what Nathan did. No say at all. But she knew in her heart that protecting Kyle too much could be as serious a problem as not protecting him enough.

Lifting the cuff of his shirt, Nathan checked his watch. "Sara has a little bit of time before she leaves. Why don't you show her your room?"

"I'd love to see your room. Maybe I could read you a story. Do you like books?"

"I like Dr. Seuss and Clifford. I even have my own Clifford. Come on, I'll show you." Quicker than lightning, Kyle scrambled off his chair and left the kitchen for a hall that must lead to the bedrooms.

Nathan pushed his chair back, stood, picked up the empty cookie dish and took it to the sink. The kitchen decor was light green and tan. The window above the sink was curtainless and void of a blind, giving an unobstructed view of the backyard. Sara had passed sliding glass doors that led out to a deck before she'd sat at the table. The wide, expansive lawn dotted with maples, sycamores and firs was inviting—for a young boy to practice pitching a baseball, or for a quiet walk to soak in the peace of nature. The sky was robin-egg blue today and cloudless. The tall firs reached up to it and were a dozen different shades of green. This was a beautiful place to raise a child. She just hoped Nathan wouldn't isolate Kyle in order to keep him safe.

"Thanks for suggesting he show me his room."

"I thought you'd like to see it."

"So I can take a mental picture of where he sleeps home with me?"

"Something like that."

When Nathan turned toward her, their gazes met, and she almost felt as if the kitchen tilted a little. That was ridiculous. She was just hyperstimulated from meeting Kyle, from holding her own with Nathan, from wanting to remember every minute so she could treasure each one in her heart always.

"Sara, come on!" Kyle's voice was enthusiastically shrill. "I want to show you my arrowheads."

Breaking eye contact with Nathan, quickly gaining her equilibrium again, she hurried down the hall to Kyle's room, knowing her time with him was limited.

* * *

Forty-five minutes later, Nathan impatiently checked his watch. He'd expected Kyle to be bored with Sara, or Sara to be bored with Kyle. He'd peeked into the room twice. The first time they were playing Candy Land. Sara had been seated cross-legged on Kyle's bed, while Kyle knelt on the floor beside it, all rapt attention as they moved their board markers according to the colors on the cards they chose. The second time he'd checked on them, he'd been surprised to see Sara on the floor. Apparently Kyle had gone through his toy chest, showing her this and that. She'd fitted his monkey puppet onto her hand and was talking in a high voice, making his son laugh.

They were getting along too well. She was bonding with Kyle. If Nathan didn't put a stop to this now, she'd want to come back. He couldn't allow that.

This time when Nathan appeared in the doorway, she was sitting on the bed again, reading Kyle a story. Her melodic voice lifted and fell, and Nathan felt almost as mesmerized as his son.

That was ridiculous. Just as ridiculous as the awareness he felt every time Sara got within two feet of him. He was on pins and needles, wishing her out of his house. That was all.

The story Sara was reading Kyle wasn't one of his usual favorites. It was *The Velveteen Rabbit*. Nathan had always considered the book too advanced for his son, but now he could see Kyle was enraptured by it—a story about a bunny loved so much it became real. Had Nathan also not pulled out that book to read at night because it would encourage his son to believe in the impossible?

The book finished, Sara closed it and saw him standing in the doorway. An expression so sad came over her face that Nathan actually felt sorry for her. Then he steeled himself against the emotion…against the compassion that would ruin what he'd built for himself and Kyle.

Colleen's pictures sat on Kyle's nightstand. What would *she* think about all this?

He pushed away that fanciful thought. "It's time for Sara to go now."

"Aw, Dad. Does she haf to?"

Although Sara looked as if she wanted to protest, too, she sat up straight. "I do have to go, Kyle. But it was a real treat visiting with you."

"Can you come back?"

Nathan rubbed his forehead. This was exactly what he'd been afraid of. "She's returning to Minneapolis tomorrow, Kyle. That's where she lives."

Sara slid her legs over the side of the bed and for a moment didn't move. Nathan wondered if she was fighting tears. He hoped not because he wouldn't know how to deal with those.

When she stood, she faced Kyle again. "My life *is* in Minneapolis. Coming up here was like a dream I had once. Thank you for making it come true."

Unexpectedly, Kyle raced around to her side of the bed and gave her a hug. "I want you to come back."

She hugged him for a very long time, then finally let

him go. "I wish I could. But sometimes we can't have what we want."

"While I walk Sara out, why don't you draw a picture of everything you did so you can give it to Gramps?"

"I want to mail it to Sara."

Nathan relented so the argument wouldn't continue. "All right, you can do that. Go ahead and get started."

Kyle gave Sara an unhappy little wave, then went over to the small table and chairs where coloring books, art paper and crayons were stacked. As he sat, he looked over his shoulder.

Nathan put his hand at the small of Sara's back and guided her out of the room. Was she trembling? Could leaving Kyle affect her this much? They didn't even know for sure if Kyle *was* her son. From what he understood, mix-ups happened in fertility clinics.

She stood silent as he pulled her jacket from the closet and handed it to her. She took it and he saw her eyes were shiny. Yet her voice was steady when she said, "Thank you for letting me meet him. I wish…" She shook her head. "You know what I wish."

"He might not even *be* your son."

"He's my son. He has my eyes."

Nathan couldn't dispute that because he saw it, too.

She crossed to the door and put her hand on the knob. "I gave you my word I'd go back to Minneapolis, and that's what I'm going to do. But if you ever change your mind about Kyle needing a mother, and if you want to find out for sure if I am or not, that's where I'll be."

As Sara left, Nathan watched her through the window. She practically ran down the walk.

She said she'd keep her word. But as he listened to her start her car, as he watched her drive away, he felt a lead weight in his chest.

If she didn't keep her word, what was he going to do?

Chapter Two

As Nathan ushered Kyle into the children's clothing store, he hoped Thanksgiving would return his son to his normal happy, active self. He'd been unusually quiet since Sara Hobart's visit.

"Boys jeans are over there." Nathan pointed to a table in the rear of the store. With winter coming on, he had realized his son had outgrown everything, from his jeans to his cold weather gear. Heavier snow was predicted for next week, over the holiday.

Kyle headed toward the back of the store with no enthusiasm at all.

Nathan knew his son hated trying on clothes. Like father, like son.

But he realized there was more to the boy's mood than an aversion to shopping for clothes. For the past week, Kyle had smiled less and seemed much too pensive. Why? Because he'd liked Sara and wanted her to visit again? Because he missed that kind of nurturing female presence in his life? Nathan had let Kyle mail her the drawings he'd made. Since then Kyle had watched the mail, as if he'd expected something from her in return. Nothing had arrived. Nathan guessed Sara believed *he* preferred she remain silent.

Over the weekend Nathan had arranged a play day with Bill Norris, a divorced dad with a six-year-old son, who attended the same church they did. Kyle had seemed to enjoy the company Saturday afternoon. Afterward, however, he'd become introspective again. Nathan had asked Kyle if something was wrong. So had his dad, as well as Val. But Kyle had just shrugged and clammed up.

As they stopped in front of the table stacked with jeans now, Nathan laid out three pairs in Kyle's size for his son to examine. "Uncle Ben said he's bringing you a surprise when he comes next Wednesday."

"Do you know what it is?" Kyle asked, looking interested.

"Nope. I have no idea."

"Is he staying lots of days?"

"Two or three."

"That's okay," Kyle replied with a grin.

Nathan was relieved to see that happy spark back in his son's eyes. He pointed to the jeans one size up from the short ones Kyle wore now. "Why don't you pick the pair you like the best. I'll check out the coats."

The boys coat rack was a few steps away. Nathan watched Kyle lift a pair of denims, flip them over and wiggle his little fingers into the back pocket.

Engrossed in trying to whittle down the selection of coats to two or three for Kyle to try on, Nathan wasn't sure he heard a low voice calling "Dad." But he turned anyway.

When he saw his son gasping for air, he dropped the coats and hurried to him. Fear shone in Kyle's eyes, and his breathing was labored.

"Hold on." Nathan tried to keep the panic from his voice as he reached for the inhaler in his pocket. Kyle hadn't suffered a serious asthma attack in over a year. That day he'd been outside playing too long, and the fall grasses had set him off.

Trying to stay calm, Nathan shook the inhaler, then held it to his son's lips. Twice Kyle sucked in the puffs of medication.

A store clerk was at Nathan's side, asking if she could help. The scent of her perfume was strong. He ignored her, all of his attention riveted on his son.

Holding the inhaler himself now, Kyle shook his head to signal the medicine wasn't helping. "I can't breathe," he rasped.

Although he realized he had to give the medication a few minutes to work, Nathan still scooped Kyle up into his arms. His boy's face was gray and he was struggling to draw in air. Waiting wasn't an option.

"Should I call emergency services?" the clerk asked.

Nathan hated watching Kyle suffer. His own pulse was racing and his heart pounded in his ears. He had to keep a clear head. If the woman called the paramedics, they would take at *least* five minutes to get here.

"Call the E.R. and tell them I'm coming—asthmatic child in crisis." Then he raced out of the store, running faster than he ever had run even when he'd sprinted in a track meet. He could be at the hospital in *less* than five minutes. Even one minute could be crucial now.

That minute could save his son's life.

As the automated doors opened for Nathan, he ran into the emergency room of Rapid Creek Community Hospital, yelling for a doctor. Although the hospital was small, it was well-equipped, with a dedicated staff. The clerk's call must have prepared them, because a doctor rushed to Nathan and showed him to a cubicle. While he administered a dose of medication, a nurse pulled the curtains around them. Kyle's lips had turned blue and his little face was ashen. Nathan prayed like he'd never prayed before.

As the doctor, whose name tag read Dr. Marshall, began Kyle's inhalation therapy, Nathan stayed by his son's side, holding his hand to keep him calm. Every few moments he said, "I'm right here. You're going to be fine."

Kyle was breathing easier now.

Dr. Marshall, who was wearing a white coat over a blue oxford shirt and khakis, looked to be in his forties. "I paged Dr. Redding."

Dr. Redding was the town's pulmonary specialist. Kyle had seen him for a checkup at the end of the summer.

"This treatment will last about ten minutes. We'll let him rest for a while, then give him another. When Dr. Redding arrives, he'll examine him thoroughly and check his blood gases. My guess is after an attack like this, he'll want to keep him overnight."

Hearing every word, Kyle's eyes widened in fear.

The doctor patted his arm. "Your dad will be able to stay if he'd like. We have a comfortable recliner he can roll next to your bed."

Nathan squeezed Kyle's hand. "If you have to stay, I'll be right here with you."

Kyle seemed to relax again at his words.

With a frown, Nathan asked, "I can't use a cell phone in the hospital, can I?"

The doctor shook his head. "No. But if you'd like us to call someone for you, I'm sure the desk nurse would be glad to do that."

"I don't want to scare my father."

"Jeannie is very good at public relations. But you will have to sign a form giving her permission to call."

"Paperwork," Nathan muttered.

"More and more every day," the doctor agreed, examining Kyle again. After studying the monitor he was hooked up to, the doctor pulled back a curtain. "I'll go get that form."

Two hours later, Nathan was seated by Kyle's bed in the pediatrics unit when his father appeared at the doorway with two cups of coffee and beckoned to him. This was his third cup of high octane caffeine. Nathan knew there'd be no sleep for him tonight. But there wouldn't have been, anyway. He'd be watching Kyle. With the oxygen tube at his son's nose and the breathing apparatus on the bedside stand, Nathan wouldn't forget why his son was here.

There was another sleeping child, a ten-year-old boy, in a bed across the room. He'd been in an accident and had his spleen removed. His parents had decided not to stay for the night.

After making sure Kyle was still sleeping, Nathan went to the door and stepped out.

Galen handed him a cup of coffee.

Nathan took off the lid and tossed it into the nearby trash can. Then he sipped it and grimaced.

"It's hot," his father warned.

"It tastes like motor oil."

"What do you expect? A latte from Javaland? I can go get you one, but I know you don't go in for that kind of thing."

"Instead of fetching coffee for me, you should just go home."

"I thought we should have a talk first."

Nathan met his dad's steel-gray eyes. "What about? What caused this episode? I spoke to his doctor. It could have been the dyes and the smells of the fabrics in the store. It could have been the clerk's perfume. It could have been—"

Galen raised a brow. "Before Kyle fell asleep, I asked him if he took his medicine this morning."

"I gave him his tablet with breakfast."

"That doesn't mean he swallowed it. And let me tell you, son, that boy can't lie any better than you could when you were a kid. He nodded that he took it, but he wouldn't look at me dead-on."

Nathan started to get angry, then reminded himself that Kyle was five years old. How could he possibly understand the gravity of his condition? "I'll have to have another talk with him. But today's scare should have been enough."

After taking a couple of swallows from his cup, Galen hooked a thumb in his suspenders and gnawed on his lower lip for a couple of seconds. "There *is* something else that could have caused this, you know."

"What?"

"Stress. Kids get stressed just like adults. You know it can be a factor in bringing on an asthma attack. Kyle's been way too quiet ever since Sara Hobart visited him. He watches the mail every day as if he expects a letter from her. That's emotional stress on the boy. Maybe you should let him know you've forbidden her from having any contact with him again, so he doesn't expect anything from her. Or…maybe you should change your mind about her visiting him again."

"You're becoming her champion?" Nathan's voice registered astonishment.

"Not *her* champion, but Kyle's. You have to do something. Who knows what ideas Kyle's imagination is spinning. He might think she doesn't want to come back…doesn't want to be friends with him."

"I never should have let her see him in the first place."

"You would have still known she was out there. When Kyle starts asking questions…"

"Why would he have questions? His mother died in childbirth. Period."

"Other folks in town know about the in vitro. You can't keep the truth hidden forever. Better Kyle knows it sooner rather than later, when he'll resent you for keeping it from him."

Nathan felt an icy chill crawl up his back. "And just what am I supposed to do about Sara Hobart? If I let her into Kyle's life, she could want more than another visit."

Holding up his hand to ward off Nathan's objections, Galen argued, "She knows she has no legal right to Kyle. But Nathan, if he *is* her son, I think you'd better consider her *moral* right." He lowered his voice. "There's a good chance she's the boy's biological mother. What if he'd died today?"

"Pop!" Nathan could feel his face go white, his entire body tense, his whole being reject the idea.

"I know that's not something you want to think about. And yes, she signed a piece of paper that says she has no rights to Kyle. No rights to make any decisions about him. No rights to visit him or hug him. I get that. Apparently she gets that, too, otherwise she wouldn't have gone back to Minneapolis. But…" Galen pointed his weathered finger at Kyle. "Just look at him, son. Look at the life he has with me and you and Val. You hardly let him go anywhere or do anything. At least can't you let someone else into his life who can love him?"

To his chagrin, Nathan could remember the happiness on Kyle's face when he'd been playing with Sara. He could remember the connection that had taken hold in a very short time. He'd wanted to deny it. He'd told himself Sara Hobart was a novelty to Kyle, and that was the reason his son liked her. But deep down, Nathan knew there was more. That "more" was what had caused the knot in his gut…the knife of fear that stabbed him every time he thought about Sara Hobart.

Galen rubbed his hand through his gray hair. "Ever since you lost Colleen, you've made Kyle the center of your world. You left your life in the city so you could come up here and make a new start with him. So you could be around for him. But maybe *you're* not enough. A dad can't be a mom. A father just doesn't know some things instinctually the way a mother does. Believe me, son, I know. Sometimes I'd dig down deep to find something to say to you or Sam or Ben and it just wasn't there."

"Obviously it wasn't there for our mother, either. Obviously she not only had nothing to say, she didn't want to say it. At least not to us. She couldn't wait to leave us and Rapid Creek. Sara Hobart has a high-powered career in Minneapolis. She's not going to leave that to take care of a little boy here. And I don't *want* her to take care of him, because *I'm* going to do that."

"Whether she's willing to be a full-time mother really isn't the issue," Galen protested. "Letting her spend a little time with Kyle is."

While Galen's words batted against Nathan's heart, he

could hear Sara's voice in his head. *I was in an accident and had to have a hysterectomy.*

His gut clenched. A coward would take the easy way out. A coward would take the safe route. A coward would forget about Sara Hobart. Forget she even existed. She had no rights, no say, no claim on his son. Yet...

Leaving his dad, Nathan walked back into Kyle's hospital room, stood by the bed and looked down at him. His son's eyes were closed, but he knew they were the same green as Sara's. Shouldn't he at least find out if she *was* Kyle's mother?

A DNA test for the three of them was a huge step, one he had to think seriously about before acting on. This wasn't the kind of decision he was impulsively going to make in the aftermath of a crisis.

Maybe tomorrow morning he'd know what to do.

Saturday afternoon, when there was a knock on Sara's office door, she looked up, expecting to see another of the firm's associates who was working on the weekend, as she was. Ever since her visit to Rapid Creek, she'd worked practically nonstop, billing more hours than she had before her accident. She hadn't known what else to do to keep her mind off Kyle.

Her gaze fell to the picture of Kyle on her desk, the one she'd taken with her camera phone. It was grainy and not very good, but it was something.

"Come in," she called, since the door didn't open at once as she'd expected it to.

When it *did* open, and she saw the man standing there, her world spun a little too fast. She wasn't dizzy, exactly, but she felt disoriented and definitely off balance. Was she seeing things?

"Can I come in?"

The deep voice was the same. The brown hair falling over his forehead was the same. The jawline Kyle had inherited was the same. Nathan Barclay stood in her office, and she was speechless.

He frowned. "I stopped by your apartment. Since it seemed deserted, I took a chance you might be working."

Finally she managed to string a few words together. "What are you doing here?"

He came further into the office. Wearing boots, jeans and a red-and-black flannel jacket, he didn't look as if he belonged in the city. "I could give you the short version or the longer version. Which would you prefer?" His gaze dropped to the photograph of Kyle on her desk. "Where did that come from?"

"My camera phone. I only took the one. I just wanted something…" She trailed off, thinking she shouldn't have to explain.

Sighing, he ran his hand through his hair. "Maybe we should do this somewhere else. How late will you be working?"

She closed the folder for the lease agreement she'd been studying. "I could be finished now if this is about Kyle."

He nodded. "It's about Kyle."

"Is anything wrong? Is he all right?"

"He's fine. Now. We need to go someplace we can talk in private. A restaurant wouldn't be a good idea."

"We can go to my place. Did you drive down from Rapid Creek?"

"No, I flew in. But I rented a car."

"Is it in the parking garage?"

"Yes."

On her visit to Rapid Creek she'd realized Nathan was a man of few words. At least with her. She wondered if he was like that with everyone, or only people he didn't know well or didn't want to know well. She got the idea his being here wasn't entirely voluntary. "I'm parked there, too. You can follow me to my place."

"That's fine," he replied, but she had the feeling that *nothing* was fine. Just why was he here?

Pushing a few files into her briefcase, she could feel his gaze on her. His appraisal made her self-conscious. When she lifted her jacket from a wooden captain's chair, she dropped it.

Close by, Nathan picked it up and handed it to her. Their gazes met and she felt impacted by the intensity in his gray eyes. She was suddenly glad he would follow her and they wouldn't be occupying the same vehicle. She needed time to compose herself and to adjust to him being here, and what that might mean.

Apparently he didn't want to discuss whatever it was on the phone. She'd expected never to see him again. Never to see Kyle again. But now a little flare of hope almost made her giddy.

Twenty minutes later Sara was letting Nathan into her apartment, trying to remember exactly what state it was in. She hadn't been there much lately, only to sleep. It was too lonely. Too quiet. But most of all, she was surrounded by too many things her mother had loved. At first after her mom died, keeping her antiques, using them herself, had felt comforting. But after Sara's accident, and after seeing Kyle, the furniture had caused her heart to ache even more.

Nathan had stopped inside the doorway and was taking it all in, from the claw-foot table and double-globed Quoizel lamp, to the lacy doilies on the arms of the camel-back sofa covered in a pretty pink flowered damask, to the Victorian lace curtains at the windows.

"What's the matter?" she asked, noticing his expression, which seemed a bit puzzled.

"This isn't at all what I expected," he admitted.

"I'm afraid to ask what you did expect." Her smile was wry and she was hoping he'd relax a little bit with her. On the other hand, it might be better if he didn't. If he relaxed she might not be able to keep her distance as well. One thing she knew about Nathan Barclay—from the pictures of his deceased wife all over his house, to his wariness about her and any claims she might have concerning Kyle—she needed to keep her distance. She'd had enough heartache in her life not to even consider giving in to a little bit of chemistry that might ripple between them.

"I expected you to live in a modern glass-and-steel condo with contemporary paintings on the walls. I never imagined lace and antiques."

"The antiques were my mother's. They weren't antiques when she bought them at yard sales and thrift shops years ago. But she had a good eye and a talent with fabric that I didn't inherit."

"You just got rid of your furniture?" he asked, quirking an eyebrow.

"Believe me, it was nothing I was attached to. Except for that rocker." She pointed to a wooden rocking chair with lions carved onto the back. "That I found for myself when I was in law school. Mom taught me how to look for bargains at yard sales. It had about ten coats of paint on it. It cleaned up great, don't you think?"

"You refinished it?"

"Sure. Lye water, steel wool, glue here and there." She headed for her kitchen, which was small but cheery, with its yellow, polished-cotton valance over the window, and philodendron hanging in one corner. "Would you like something to drink? Tea or coffee?"

"Coffee."

A long counter separated the living room from the kitchen, with a post at each end rising to the ceiling. After taking off her jacket and hanging it over a dining room chair, she quickly poured water into the tank of the coffeepot. She measured out chocolate-flavored coffee, which was all she had, and switched the pot on.

Sneaking a glance at Nathan, she noticed him unzip his jacket and lay it over the back of the sofa. He wandered about, studying the titles on her bookshelves. A duplicate picture of Kyle sat on the coffee table. She felt…naked having his dad look around her place like this. Intuition told her he was absorbing everything he could about her. She didn't know if that was a good thing or not.

Producing a copper tray from a cupboard, she set two mugs of coffee on it, a carton of nonfat creamer, and sugar packets she kept for guests. Then she carried it to the coffee table and lowered herself to the sofa cushion, hoping Nathan would sit, too. He was making her jittery just being here.

But if she thought she was jittery before, when he came over and sat beside her, she knew the true meaning of the word. When she'd visited Rapid Creek, she'd attributed her reaction to him to the situation, meeting Kyle for the first time and being stirred up about all of it. Now, however, she realized the man himself disturbed her... made her suddenly feel...hot.

Pouring a liberal amount of creamer into her mug, she picked it up, took a few bolstering sips, then set it on a coaster. "So tell me why you're here."

She was half afraid he was going to tell her he was having a restraining order placed upon her, so that she wouldn't come anywhere near him or Kyle. But maybe that was just the lawyer in her being paranoid.

"I came to ask you to spend Thanksgiving with us in Rapid Creek."

Nothing he might have said could have surprised her more. "You want me to spend Thanksgiving with you and Kyle?" She had to clarify so she was sure she hadn't misunderstood.

"This isn't what I want," he told her bluntly, "but I think it's necessary. We need to have DNA testing done to find out if you're Kyle's mother."

"Why is this necessary now, when it wasn't ten days ago? In fact, you didn't want me anywhere around. Why the about-face?"

After a few beats of silence, he replied, "Because Kyle had a serious asthma attack. He could have died."

"Oh, my Lord." She felt the color drain from her face as the reality of his words sunk in.

Nathan swore. "I shouldn't have said it like that."

Although he might not want to admit it, she could see he was still upset by whatever had occurred. "Tell me what happened."

"Kyle has never had an attack this serious before. He had the one when he was three...one last year...but nothing since. Just wheezing sometimes." He told her about taking Kyle to the store to buy clothes, the possibility of fabric smells or perfume setting off the attack.

"You didn't say anything about perfume when I came to visit."

"You weren't wearing any."

No, she wasn't. Because perfume bothered some of her clients, she was careful about the products she chose. But the fact that Nathan Barclay had noticed that...well, of course he would have noticed if he was protective of Kyle.

"So you don't know for sure what caused it?"

"My father has another theory."

"And that is?"

"Kyle has been different, more quiet, more subdued since your visit. Dad feels there was an unconscious connection between the two of you and Kyle felt the loss of that. He looked for something from you in the mail every day. Emotional stress can be a component in an asthma attack."

"You didn't want me to have any contact! You told me not to write…to stay out of Kyle's life."

"I know. Possibly I was wrong. Maybe I underestimated his need of a woman your age in his life."

"You don't believe we had a connection because I'm his mother and he's my son?"

"We don't know that. I don't believe you two bonded because of some mystical mother-son thread. You played with Kyle…with his fire trucks. You read him stories. Why wouldn't he like you?"

"Mr. Barclay—"

"It's Nathan," he said curtly. "If we're going to be around each other, if you're going to be under my roof, we might as well be on a first-name basis."

"You want me to stay in your house rather than the lodge?" she asked in astonishment.

"The whole point of this is for you to spend time with Kyle, isn't it?"

"And if I'm *not* his mother?"

"Then he'll have made a new friend. You can write to him and he can write back, and we can all relax."

Was this really so simple for him? "When are you returning to Rapid Creek?"

"Tomorrow morning. I don't want to be away too long.

The doctor changed Kyle's medication, and he seems to be doing fine. But I don't want to take any chances."

She did some quick calculating, weighing pros and cons, responsibility in her job against responsibility for a boy who could be her son. "I can't fly back with you tomorrow. But I think I'll be able to arrange everything by Tuesday. Would that be all right?"

"Tuesday would work out well. My brother Ben is flying in Wednesday night. We can keep Kyle's excitement to small doses."

Sara wondered again if Nathan was trying to protect Kyle a little too much…and if that might not be the basis of the whole problem. But she couldn't put forth that theory until she learned more about Kyle and Nathan, how they related, and more about asthma itself. On the other hand, Nathan probably wouldn't want to hear what she thought about it. Even if she *was* Kyle's biological mother, she still had no legal claim, no parental claim, because of the release form she'd signed. She had to simply try to keep everything on an even keel with Nathan and not upset the proverbial apple cart. Most important, she had to prove she could be a healthy influence in Kyle's life. In addition, she'd like to get a handle on Nathan. Try to get to know him a little better before she landed on his turf again.

She asked, "Did you check into a motel?"

"Not yet. Why?"

"Because I have a spare bedroom. You're welcome to sleep here tonight if you'd like. If I'm going to be spending time at your house, it only seems fair."

His eyes locked on hers. "Are you sure you want a houseguest on such short notice?"

Trying to lighten the atmosphere a bit, she smiled. "I was a Girl Scout. I'm always prepared. I have extra towels, a new bar of soap and clean sheets on the guest room bed. Your staying will be no trouble at all."

Yet as she noticed the intensity in his dark eyes, the beard stubble lining his jaw, the lines around his mouth and his taut, nicely shaped lips, she suddenly realized inviting him to stay the night could cause her trouble with a capital T.

Her heart sped up while she waited for his answer, and she didn't know whether to hope he'd accept her offer or leave for a motel!

Chapter Three

As Nathan stared up at the ceiling of Sara's spare room, with the subtle scent of lavender escaping from a dish on the dresser, he reminded himself again that staying here was the practical and convenient thing to do. After all, he'd be leaving first thing in the morning. What did it matter where he bedded down for the night?

It mattered.

When he'd accepted her invitation, she'd told him straight out that she wouldn't bother him, that he could pretend he was staying at a hotel, that she had some work to do on her computer in her bedroom and he could make himself a sandwich, open the package of cookies on the counter, help himself to whatever he could find.

That's what he'd done, and he'd turned in early.

Levering himself up in the double bed now, he switched on the bedside lamp. He felt so out of place here. This *wasn't* a motel. The furniture wasn't impersonal. Sara had told him this brass bed had been hers when she was a child. The blue-and-white-striped spread and coordinating curtains were obviously new. But the snow globe with the castle on the dresser, the photograph of Sara and her mother in the crystal frame on the nightstand, the faded latch-hook rug with butterflies and flowers next to the bed, were belongings Sara clearly cherished.

He realized he was trying to get to know this woman without actually getting to know her. Maybe he was just searching for signs or signals that would warn him if there were dangerous waters ahead. His eyes fell on the paperback thriller poking out of his duffel bag. But then his stomach grumbled. He might as well get something to eat and spend the next hour reading. Maybe then he could doze off.

Listening for a moment, he didn't hear a sound in the apartment, and suspected Sara was already sound asleep.

He'd brought navy flannel sleeping shorts for his overnight stay. He hadn't figured he'd need anything else, alone in a motel room. He *could* put on his jeans. Nah. He'd be in and out of the kitchen in a couple of minutes.

When he passed Sara's room, he was relieved to see no light shone under the door. He switched on the hall light soundlessly, then went down the short corridor to the dining room. As he passed through it, he saw the hood light glowing over the stove in the kitchen. At the same moment, he realized Sara was standing at the sink, likely as startled to see him as he was to see her. She was wearing a fuchsia nightshirt with Peace embroidered across the front in sparkly letters. The sleeves went to her elbows, while the V-neck hinted at her cleavage.

He quickly pulled his gaze up to her face, but that wasn't a whole lot better. Her blond hair was tousled. Her big green eyes were wide with surprise. Devoid of makeup, her flawless skin asked to be touched.

He stopped, not sure whether to proceed or retreat. Her gaze was glued to his bare chest for a moment, then dropped lower, to the elastic band on his shorts. His equilibrium went haywire.

Finally, her eyes meeting his, her cheeks a little flushed, she said, "I thought you'd be sleeping."

"And I thought *you'd* be sleeping."

"You need another pillow or comforter or—?"

"No, Sara. I'm just fine." Then he said the first thing that came into his head. "My stomach was grumbling."

Her hand fluttered toward the refrigerator. "Help yourself. There's still plenty of sandwich fixings. I'm trying warm milk. Want some?"

He wrinkled his nose. "That idea never appealed to me."

She laughed, and the sound awakened something in his heart, something shadowy that had been lost since Colleen had died.

"You have to add a little honey and a square of chocolate so that it becomes a magic sleeping potion," she said.

He chuckled. "Magic is right."

"Don't turn up your nose if you haven't tried it."

There was something completely unpretentious about Sara that he couldn't help but like. "I'll pass for tonight."

Opening the refrigerator, he pulled out a package of ham, along with cheese, and grabbed the mustard and a head of lettuce. When he took the items to the counter, Sara passed him the loaf of bread. He could tell she wasn't wearing a bra under the nightshirt. Why would she, to sleep?

Since that thought almost made him break into a sweat, he concentrated on making sandwiches. "Want one?" he asked as she stood there, silently stirring her milk.

"No, thanks. If I make a sandwich and sleep on it, I'll be wearing a few extra pounds in the morning."

Before he thought better of it, he muttered, "I doubt that."

She looked surprised at his comment and her cheeks became a little pinker. Switching off the burner, she poured her milk concoction into a mug. "Do you want to eat alone or do you want company?"

Although he'd rather just take his sandwiches to his room and dive into the thriller—that was the *safe* thing to do—he thought a little conversation might be a good tactic before Sara actually moved into his house for a couple of days. The only problem was, that damn V-neckline distracted him.

"Company's fine. Maybe we'll both be able to sleep when we're finished," he decided.

When he took the plate of sandwiches to the table, she followed, and he had the feeling she was inspecting him as they walked. What a weird sensation that gave him. How long had it been since a woman checked him out? He supposed turnabout was fair play, but the idea was arousing. He quickly sat at the table.

After she set her mug at the place mat, she went back to the refrigerator, pulled out a carton of orange juice and snagged a glass from the cupboard.

"Thanks," he murmured, wondering if her thoughtfulness was a part of who she was or a part she played whenever she had a guest. He wondered if she had guests often…especially men guests.

Seated around the corner from him, she crossed her legs under the table. Her toes brushed his ankle and a jolt of fire leaped up his leg.

She looked a bit embarrassed as she shifted to the far edge of her chair, putting more distance between them. "So is the article I read about you accurate?" she asked. "Were you a financial analyst once upon a time?"

"Yes, I was. I was with an investment banking firm. I was on the fast track to becoming a rich, powerful mover and shaker."

He'd said it so tongue-in-cheek, she laughed. "You didn't want all that?"

"Back then I wanted it…before I knew what was really important."

Her eyes were wide again. "What did you find that was really important?"

"When I got married, I knew my marriage was important, but I think my job was still at the top of the list. I was headed up and nothing was going to stop me."

She stirred her hot milk. "Kyle's birth did?"

Obviously, she was tiptoeing around the death of Colleen and Kyle's twin. Hesitating before he answered, he finally admitted, "Not Kyle's birth. The attempts to have a child. Most couples take the whole process for granted…at least, I always did. I figured I'd get married someday, have kids, send them to college, retire and enjoy life. But Colleen and I hit a roadblock right out of the gate. She was thirty-two when we started trying to have kids, and we didn't think there would be a problem. But after two years, she still wasn't pregnant. We both had all kinds of testing done. At age thirty-four then, she had an elevated follicle stimulating hormone level. The specialist told us as she grew older and those levels rose, the likelihood of having genetically abnormal eggs also escalated. So we decided to try in vitro with an egg donor."

He'd thought about this over and over…analyzed every step. "Going back over everything that happened, I wonder if we weren't meant to be childless. The testing, the in vitro, was tough on our marriage. When Colleen stroked out during the delivery process, I felt as if we'd gone against fate or something."

Gazing into Sara's eyes, he saw that she understood, maybe because of the losses she'd suffered.

She reached out and touched his hand. "You can't think that."

The contact was like fire, and he jerked his hand away. He'd loved his wife, but here he was, talking about her and his marriage, yet feeling some sort of chemistry with this woman he didn't even know.

He bet the chemistry would quit when he questioned her about the money she received for donating her eggs. Maybe she did it to subsidize her high-powered career.

"Why did you donate your eggs? Did you need the money for college?" He tried to keep his voice non-judgmental. She might tell him it was none of his business.

She looked down at her hands and for a moment he thought maybe she felt guilty about it. After all, she could have used the ten thousand on a new car.

But then Sarah lifted her gaze to his, and the emotion in her eyes told him something else was coming…something he never expected.

"My mom became ill. She needed a bone marrow transplant but that treatment was considered experimental with her condition. Her insurance company wouldn't pay."

"Ten thousand dollars wouldn't be nearly enough for that!"

"No, it wasn't. But our church began holding fundraisers. It seemed everyone in town wanted to help. But even with that, we were short on the down payment. The money I received along with the rest enabled my mom to start treatment."

He'd been wrong about Sara's motives and so had Ben. Chances were good they'd wanted to think the worst of her. That would make the whole situation easier…easier to push her out of Kyle's life. But the woman before him had been willing to sacrifice for her mother. And after all that, tragedy had struck again.

"Tell me about your accident," he requested gently.

"Do you really want to know the details?"

No, he didn't. But for some reason he felt it was essential he gathered *all* the facts about Sara Hobart. Maybe he could figure her out then *and* what she truly wanted.

"Does it bother you to talk about it?"

"No." She amended her answer. "Yes. Just when I think I've put it behind me, I remember I can never have children and it's all there again."

"I read the account of it on the Internet," he admitted.

"It's so cut and dry in the newspaper, isn't it? A driver under the influence of cold medication passed out, jumped the median strip and plowed into me." She took a deep breath. "I'm lucky to be alive. Lucky I don't remember the actual accident or the ambulance trip to the hospital. But I remember everything from surgery on. Most of all, when the doctor told me he had to perform a hysterectomy."

Nathan knew how much *he'd* wanted to be a dad. What if he'd gone to bed one night and awakened in the morning to a stranger telling him he could never father a child. He could hardly imagine how devastated Sara must have been.

Sara rearranged herself in her chair, took a few swallows of her milk and then admitted, "When I donated my eggs in exchange for the money, I didn't know if it was the right thing to do. I know the money was supposed to compensate me for my time, the physical distress to my body and all of that, but taking it bothered me. Still, it pro-longed my mom's life for five years. I had all these extra days and hours and minutes to spend with her. I'll never regret that."

"I think I hear a 'but,'" Nathan replied gruffly.

"My career had always been my ambition, my vocation, my life. It gave me energy and purpose even throughout mom's illness. Because of it, we could keep up with the bills and I could give mom what she needed. I could focus on a business that had somehow gotten into trouble—either with a lawsuit against it or red tape tangles—and escape for a time before I had to face the fact again that mom was slipping away. But…after my accident and the hysterec-tomy, like you, I tried to find meaning in everything that had happened, and I couldn't. My career didn't mean what it had before. It was all just too confusing to try to figure out. And I had to know if I had a child out there."

Although he wanted to separate himself from Sara and her interference in his life, he could understand her rea-soning and her longing. Nathan ate his sandwiches in silence. Once in a while, she sipped her milk, looked over at him, then glanced away.

He had the feeling they'd shared a little bit too much personal information too soon. He never talked to anyone about Colleen, what they'd gone through, what he'd felt after she and Mark had died. Why now? Why this woman?

Because she might be Kyle's mother.

No matter how much he wanted to eradicate that fact, he kept bumping into it.

Finished eating, he stood and took his dish and glass over to the sink. Sara did the same. Unfortunately, they reached for the handle to the dishwasher at the same time. Their fingers tangled and this time neither of them pulled away. When Nathan gazed into her eyes, he felt a churning inside of him. It was uncomfortable, unwelcome and totally unsettling. He was standing bare chested and barefoot, with only sleeping shorts between him and her cotton nightshirt. The impulse to kiss her was so strong he had to close his eyes. He took a step back, and when he opened them again, he saw she had done the same thing. She was standing in the corner, both hands around her mug.

He opened the dishwasher, dropped in his plate and glass and waited for her to put her mug in.

"I have to rinse it," she said softly.

When he lifted the door to close it, he didn't step away fast enough. The next second she was there at the sink beside him, his body practically touching hers. She didn't wear perfume, yet she did use a shampoo that smelled fruity. Standing this close, looking down at her, he found his gaze going to the V between her breasts under the nightshirt. He knew he should look away. He really should. But he hadn't gazed at a woman in an intimate way in five long years. His desire and passion and need had been frozen. Now it all woke up and practically bowled him over.

Sara was biting her lower lip, and he was fighting for…what? Control? Composure? Propriety? He swallowed, mentally pouring freezing water over his libido, and turned away from her.

"I'll be leaving for the airport around seven," he called over his shoulder.

"Nathan?"

He stopped, and politeness made him face her again. "What?"

"Would you like me to make breakfast?"

"No. I'll grab a bagel at the airport. Why don't you just stay in bed." It was more than a suggestion; it was practically an order.

Although he didn't think she was the type of woman who took orders, she nodded. "That would probably be best."

As she turned on the spigot, he strode quickly to his bedroom. He had a feeling he'd finish that novel tonight, because he sure as hell wasn't going to get any sleep.

Sara was transferring file folders from her desk to her briefcase when Ted Feeney knocked on her open door Monday evening. Whenever she saw Ted, her heart still hurt a little. Not because she wanted to date him again. She'd learned what kind of man he really was. But her heart hurt because of the dreams he'd represented...the ones she'd had to bury. They hadn't talked for weeks, not since he'd admitted a woman who couldn't have children didn't fit into his life plan.

So why was he here now?

She forced a smile. After all, they worked for the same firm. "Hi, Ted."

"I heard you're taking time off again." He was trying for a nonchalant tone, but she heard an edge of disapproval underneath.

What she did was none of his business. Not any more. Although they'd dated for a few months, she'd realized after her accident that she hadn't really known him. He'd been charming to her at work and whenever they'd dated. He'd been a caring lover. She'd respected his lawyer-on-the-rise attitude. But he had his mind rigidly fixed on what he wanted in life and he wouldn't veer from that. He wanted a woman who could provide him with his own children. Case closed.

She answered his query. "Yes, I am taking some time off."

"Just for the holiday?"

"I'm not sure. I've requested a leave for a few weeks."

"Do you think that's wise?"

She stopped filling her briefcase. "Wise?" Just what was Ted concerned about?

"You've worked harder than any of the associates since you've been hired on, put in more hours. You've built up capital. You don't want to lose all that now, do you?"

She wondered where his concern was coming from. Maybe he thought he'd been too blunt with her when they'd broken up?

"Something has come up that I need to take care of. I'm not sure how long it will take." She didn't know why she was explaining to him. Maybe because once upon a time she'd thought they could have a future together.

Frowning now, he kept pushing. "Are you looking

around for another position? Is that what this is about? Are you interviewing? Because if you are, the higher-ups will get wind of it and you'll be out of here quicker than—"

She held up her hand to stop his interrogation. "Ted, I'm not looking for another job. This is something personal and I can't handle it long distance."

That surprised him. "Long distance?"

"Betty will have an address and number where she can reach me, and I have my cell phone. I'm not going to be incommunicado. Just away."

Regrouping, he thought about it, then asked, "Will you be back for the round of holiday parties?"

Usually the firm threw a Christmas party. In addition, the managing partners had holiday celebrations in their homes. "I don't know. Why?"

He looked a bit chagrined at her question. "Well…I'm not dating anyone right now and I thought maybe we could catch a cab together."

Catch a cab together? She almost laughed at his choice of words. "Why? You're not interested in anything serious with me. What would be the point?" she asked, choosing bluntness to get to the bottom of this inquisition.

"I like you, Sara. I always have. I've missed you…especially in bed. There's no reason why we can't enjoy the party circuit over the holidays together, is there?"

"You want to sleep with me until you find a suitable partner?"

"Is there anything wrong with that?"

"For me, there is. You and I…I don't even know if we can still be friends."

"Sara—"

She wasn't getting into this now, not when her trip to Rapid Creek was on her mind, not when she was hoping beyond hope that Kyle was her son. Wouldn't Ted just love *that* turn of events.

Clicking her briefcase shut, she took her coat from the brass tree and slipped it on over her suit.

Ted sighed and preceded her out of her office.

She closed the door.

Politely, she said, "Thanks for thinking about me, Ted, but right now I don't know what the next few weeks are going to bring. In the meantime, you have a great Thanksgiving."

"You, too," he called as she walked down the hall and headed for the elevators.

Inviting Sara Hobart to Rapid Creek wasn't the smartest thing he'd ever done, Nathan decided, as he hung the wreath Val had made on the front door the Tuesday before Thanksgiving. How would Sara being here change the holiday? How would her presence affect Kyle?

The answers to those questions eluded him as he heard a vehicle roll up the drive. It was his brother Sam's van. As always, Patches, a mutt—brown, white and tan, and the size of a Labrador retriever—sat in the passenger seat, peering out the window. His one ear stood up, the other flopped over. Patches was his brother's best friend.

Sam hopped out of the silver vehicle and commanded Patches to stay. The dog did.

Nathan glimpsed the cartons packed in the passenger seats, the snowshoes wedged between them, the skis on the rack on top.

As Sam strode up the walk, his brown hair lifted in the wind. His blue down jacket was unzipped and his jeans were worn.

Nathan got a bad feeling in his gut.

As Sam approached, he stepped away from the door. "Are you on your way somewhere?" he asked.

"I am. And I don't want an argument from you. I'm on my way to the cabin."

The cabin was a place their dad had invested in after his divorce. It was sturdy, built of logs, and didn't have a lot of conveniences, except a wood stove insert for the fireplace, electricity and running water. Other than that, it held good memories. It had been a place Nathan, his two brothers and his father had gone, all of them confused, after Nathan's mother's defection. They'd found laughter again there. They'd fished in the nearby lake, waded in the creek in the back and hiked until they were too tired to think about the fact they no longer had a mom.

"Why now? You're going to miss Thanksgiving."

"That's the idea. Ben's coming in tomorrow night and Dad's still patting my shoulder, telling me I'll get over Alicia. I've been snapping at Eric all week. The concerned look in Corrie's eyes just makes me want to shut the office door and lock them all out."

Eric was Sam's partner at Meadowbrook Veterinary Clinic in Rapid Creek. Corrie was a vet tech who had worked for them for a couple of years.

"You think going away will help?"

"I'm not just going to be spending Thanksgiving away. I'll be staying up there for a while—to ice fish, cross-country ski and do some research. I need to block out the world."

"How long?"

"I don't know yet. When I come back, I come back. I'm not going to say goodbye to Dad, because I don't want to make long explanations. You're going to be the spokesperson, so do a good job of it and tell everyone just to leave me alone."

"Can Eric handle the clinic on his own?"

"It's slower this time of year than in the spring, summer and fall. Corrie's a big help. I've contacted Doc Merkle. He said he'll come out of retirement if Eric needs him while I'm away. So we're covered."

Sam and Eric had bought the clinic from Dr. Merkle after they'd graduated from veterinary school. They'd gone in hock up to their eyebrows, but the veterinary practice was a success and they were closing the gap.

"Look. I know Alicia really axed you. But do you really want to miss the holidays with us?"

"The truth is, Nathan, the holidays make me think of kids. I love being around Kyle, but it just hurts too much now. And knowing Alicia aborted our baby just about kills me every time I think about it. Here, I can't get away from toys in shop windows, Santa Claus peering down from the lamppost in the square and Christmas trees decorated with toy drums. I need this time. So give it to me, okay?"

In the van, Patches barked.

Sam waved to him and called, "I'm coming." Returning his attention to Nathan, he explained, "I want to reach the cabin before dark so I can check everything. I've gotta shove off." He turned to go.

"Sam?"

His brother swung around.

Nathan reached out a hand. Sam grasped it and they slapped each other on the back. "I'll do my best to explain this to Dad and Ben," Nathan assured him. "But Kyle's going to be a little tougher."

"Just tell him when I finally do come home, I'll let him spend a night with me and Patches."

To Nathan's surprise, when Kyle had been tested for allergies, he showed no sensitivity to animals. That was a good thing, because he loved being around Patches as well as Sam.

"I'll tell him. But delayed gratification doesn't go over well with kids."

"It will give him something to look forward to."

Since Sam had been mostly incommunicado the past couple of weeks, Nathan hadn't told him about Sara's visit and his flight to Minneapolis to invite her to Rapid Creek for Thanksgiving. His brother had enough on his mind. By the time he returned to Rapid Creek, maybe everything with Sara would be resolved.

But as Sam drove away, Nathan realized there was only

one resolution he wanted. He wanted the DNA test sample to prove Sara Hobart was *not* Kyle's mother.

Yet, for his son's sake, could he really wish for that?

The results of the DNA test would carve out their road to the future. He didn't like not controlling his own destiny.

He didn't like it one bit.

As Sara descended the steps of the commuter plane, the late November wind buffeted the travel bag that held her computer. She and Nathan hadn't talked about exactly how long she was going to stay, but she knew DNA testing with private labs took about two weeks. If he didn't want her in his house that long, she'd make other arrangements.

And if she *was* Kyle's mother?

All the possibilities swirled in her head. She had to make a living. She couldn't give up her job in Minneapolis, could she?

Those kinds of questions kept her awake at night and served no useful purpose right now. Just as her dreams of Nathan the past few nights served no useful purpose. She was deluding herself if she thought he was interested in her. She was deluding herself if she thought she should be interested in him. He was nine years, a marriage and a lifetime of experiences older than she was. They had *nothing* in common.

Except maybe for Kyle.

As she hurried across the tarmac to get out of the cold, she followed other passengers into the Rapid Creek terminal.

The airport wasn't very large and she spotted the baggage claim right away, expecting to see Nathan somewhere nearby. She hadn't talked with him directly. She'd left a message as to what time she'd be getting in. If he hadn't gotten it, she'd have to call him again.

A few minutes later, her bag was rounding the corner on the conveyer belt when she saw a tall, gray-haired and balding man approaching her. "Sara Hobart?"

She nodded.

With a smile, he asked, "Is that yours?"

"Yes, but—"

Reaching for her bag, he yanked the suitcase from the conveyer belt and held it by his side. Extending his other hand, he introduced himself. "I'm Galen Barclay."

Sara had been curious about Nathan's father, and now she'd have a chance to have that satisfied. But she wondered why Nathan hadn't come himself.

Balancing her suitcase easily, the older man explained, "Nathan wanted to spend the evening with Kyle. He asked if I'd come fetch you."

She wondered if that was the only reason. Or if he guessed spending time alone in the car with her could be as tense as their last encounter. "It's a pleasure to meet you, Mr. Barclay," she said as she shook his hand. "Does the lodge have many guests over the holiday?"

"We're full up." Appraising her outfit, he remarked, "Glad to see you dressed for the weather."

She'd worn her white-and-red down parka, black corduroy slacks with a black turtleneck sweater, and black boots. "I left my suits and high heels back in Minneapolis," she teased, wondering what Nathan had told his father about her.

"You have a sense of humor! You're going to need it around my son."

As he started walking and she followed, she asked, "Nathan has brothers, right?"

"He has two, both younger. You'll meet Ben tomorrow night when he flies in from Albuquerque."

When Galen didn't elaborate on his third son, she wondered why.

The parking lot attached to the airport was simple to navigate. As they walked, he mumbled, "I guess I should have offered to bring the car over to the door."

"I like exercise, Mr. Barclay. I'm fine."

He stopped and gave her another assessing look. Then he said, "It's Galen."

"And call me Sara," she offered.

With a short nod, he took off again with long athletic strides a lot like Nathan's.

After she was seated in a van that had Pine Grove Lodge printed on its side, she commented, "It's going to feel funny being here without a car. Is there anyplace I can rent one?"

"No need for you to do that. Besides the lodge's van, I have my own car. Nathan has an SUV and a pickup. Can you drive a stick shift?"

"My first car was a stick."

"Good. Then you can drive the pickup."

"Nathan might not—"

"Nathan always sees the practical side. He'll let you use it."

Taking a chance, she decided to try to get some facts out of Galen Barclay. "Is it because Nathan's practical that he wants to do this DNA test?"

"You mean because he doesn't want you popping up sometime, demanding it?"

"Yes."

He turned on the heater full blast. "That's part of it, I guess, but there are lots of other reasons, too. He and his brothers didn't have a mom for most of their lives. He saw how Kyle related to you, and it got to him, whether he'll admit it or not. Then there's the asthma attack Kyle had. I didn't see it happen, but it must have been pretty rough. I think it just emphasized the fact that life's short and maybe Nathan needs to give Kyle more than a good material life. Do you know what I mean?"

"I think so. But I know he doesn't want me here."

Galen glanced at her, then shrugged. "Maybe not. Still, he knows this test is the right thing to do."

The right thing to do. To Nathan Barclay, that's what this test was. To her, it was so much more.

Within ten minutes, they'd turned off the main road onto a lane that wound past a lake and through fir trees. When they arrived at the lodge, Sara couldn't see much in the dark, but she remembered everything about it, from the gables and stone face to its three stories and double hung windows. As Galen passed the lodge, and a lot where guests parked, her gaze focused on a light ahead of them.

At the walk to Nathan's log home, Galen switched off the ignition. Sara opened her door and climbed out, automatically going to the back to get her luggage. She'd opened the door and was pulling out her computer bag and suitcase when Galen asked, "What are you doing?"

"Getting my luggage," she responded with a smile.

"You're our guest. I'll take those."

"I'm not really a guest. More like an unasked for visitor." She had to admit that out loud so they all knew where they stood.

"Maybe so, but I'll still take the suitcase."

Seeing that this was a matter of pride for the older man, Sara let him have the bag and then walked up the sidewalk with him. Galen opened the door without knocking, then stepped into the living room. Kyle was sitting on the sofa beside Nathan, watching a DVD. When the boy saw Sara, he whooped and came running to her, throwing his arms around her legs.

"Sara! You came back."

Swallowing hard, her heart aching with affection and churning with questions, she crouched down in front of him. "I'm going to spend Thanksgiving with you. How about that?" She looked up at Nathan to see if he'd given any other explanation. Her pulse raced as she looked into his eyes.

"I didn't tell Kyle you were coming in case you couldn't get away."

In case she couldn't get away? Not likely.

Galen set down her luggage. "I had to practically wrestle her suitcase from her. I don't know what it is about women today who think they have to do it all."

Sara thought she heard some bitterness in Galen's voice, but it was gone when he asked Kyle, "How about if we make some popcorn before you go to bed?"

"I want Sara to play with my fire trucks and read me a story."

"It's getting late for more playing," Nathan told his son. "But if Sara's not too tired, she might read you a story."

Kyle looked up at her with big green eyes and a hopeful smile. "Are you too tired?"

"Not at all. You can pick one out while I unpack."

When Kyle ran to his room to do just that, Nathan shook his head. "I'd like to bottle some of that energy." He lifted her suitcase and gestured down the hall. "Come on, I'll show you to your room."

Following him, she felt as if she'd just stepped into a parallel life drastically different from her own.

At the doorway to the spare room, they paused, and their gazes met. "I'm afraid this one is a lot more sparse than the room in your apartment." Nathan's voice was gruff, and she wondered if he was concerned that she was judging his house and maybe his life with his son.

As she stepped into the bedroom, she found it *was* sparse. There was a lodgepole-pine bed with a hunter-green coverlet, a light pine dresser and nightstand. Wooden blinds were pulled and shut over the windows. On the plank flooring, a braided rug lay on one side of the bed. Yes, the room was sparse, but it was charming in its Minnesota-woods way. She liked it.

Nathan set her suitcase on the floor while she carried her computer bag to the bed. It was high. Hopping onto it, she bounced a little. "This is great."

"You'll have to share a bathroom with Kyle. I have one in the master suite."

"I won't mind, if he doesn't."

"You'll mind if you get into the bathtub to take a shower and you slip on one of his toys. Make sure his boats aren't in the bottom before you get in."

Pushing up from the bed, she stood and came over to where he was standing at the dresser. "Nathan, if you really don't want a houseguest, I could stay in town again."

"Would you feel more comfortable there?"

She could see he wanted an honest answer. "No, I want to be around Kyle rather than running back and forth. But it's your call."

"I invited you to stay here. Let's just leave it at that."

"There *could* be some advantages to me staying here," she suggested with a smile. "What are you doing for Thanksgiving dinner?"

"I was going to order plates from the lodge restaurant."

"Would you rather I cook?"

Her suggestion surprised him. "You know how to roast a turkey?"

"My mom was a great cook. She taught me the basics,

and a holiday turkey was one of them. I can even make chestnut stuffing. Is there a fresh market anywhere around here? Are they open before Thanksgiving?"

"I think there's one that's open on Wednesdays and Saturdays in the old warehouse on the edge of town. I haven't been there in years. I shop at the grocery store."

"If you haven't been there for a while, you're probably in for a treat. Do you think I could still get a turkey there?"

Nathan shrugged. "It's possible. If not, I'll show you the poultry department in the grocery store."

He gave her a genuine smile and Sara's knees felt a bit wobbly. That was ridiculous. She couldn't feel weak from a man's smile. She was just tired from racing around for the past two days.

"Can we take Kyle along?" she asked.

"We'll have to…unless Dad can watch him. I gave the housekeeper time off until Monday. Ben's flying in tomorrow night. How far can we stretch the turkey?"

"I'm thinking maybe a fifteen-pound bird. You can invite whoever you want. There'll be enough for your dad, your brother and probably a few guests."

"I think we'll bypass the few guests, but Dad and Ben won't turn down a home-cooked meal. When Val's off, Kyle and I usually live on hash, hamburgers and scrambled eggs."

"And Kyle probably loves it."

"Yeah, I think he does. Val leaves casseroles for the weekend, but sometimes we do our own thing."

Nathan was wearing a flannel shirt, jeans and boots

tonight, and looked more relaxed than she'd ever seen him. Maybe because he was on his home turf. Maybe because he didn't feel as threatened by her.

The smell of popcorn wafted down the hall. "We'd better get some of that before there isn't any left. Kyle dives into it with both hands," Nathan said.

She was intending to move past him when he caught her arm. Going still, she looked up. Suddenly neither of them were relaxed anymore. His hand on her arm created a connection she felt to her toes.

Releasing her, he stepped back. "I just wanted to tell you I made an appointment with Kyle's doctor for Friday morning. He'll take the samples for the DNA testing then."

"All right." She might as well tell him now that she was going to stay until she knew for sure whether she was Kyle's mother or not. "I took a leave of absence to stay in Rapid Creek until we know the results of the tests. As I said before, if you don't want me here, I'll find a place in town."

"Can you afford to take a leave?"

"All I do is work, Nathan. I received an insurance settlement from the accident that paid off my school loans. So I'll be fine. If I do stay here with you, I want to pay you something."

"No, absolutely not."

"Nathan…"

"No, Sara. I won't take money from you. Somehow we'll figure out how all of this is going to work out. For now, let's just get through Thanksgiving."

She wanted to do more than just get through Thanksgiving. Maybe she could make this a holiday for both Kyle and Nathan to remember.

As she followed Nathan into the hall, she felt totally out of her element. She was used to planning her life, not randomly going with the flow. Still, something felt right about her being here in Rapid Creek right now.

For once in her life, she was going to try to stop planning and just live.

Chapter Four

"We're lucky Sara's making Thanksgiving dinner." Kyle was still exuberant about her arrival.

She had just shown him how to choose the ripest tomato from the stack at a stand in the market.

At this moment, Sara felt lucky and blessed, but scared, too. Whatever this attraction was between her and Nathan could complicate her relationship with Kyle. At breakfast this morning, she and Nathan had been...polite. Nathan had informed her the market was open from 6:00 a.m. until 3:00 p.m., so they could leave whenever they were ready. He'd intended to have his dad watch Kyle, but when his son had asked, "Can I go along, too?" and Nathan couldn't come up with a good reason why he shouldn't, the outing was born.

Kyle picked out another tomato redder than the others and handed it to Sara. Again she smiled at him and winked. "You're so good at tomatoes, let's try broccoli. Pick out a big bunch with no yellow."

Kyle did so, while both adults looked on. Sara's pulse raced with Nathan close by. She had the feeling his focus was on her as much as on Kyle.

A few minutes later she was leading the procession when she came to a case of turkey products. "No turkeys left?" she asked the proprietor, who stood behind the refrigerated case.

"Not a one."

"I think you have one set aside for us." Nathan's deep voice came from behind her shoulder. "I phoned you this morning. Barclay."

"Oh, sure. You called me soon after the sun came up. Good thing, too. Most of my turkeys were spoken for." He turned around and opened the chest refrigerator behind him, lifting out a huge bag. "It's a fifteen pounder, just like you asked for."

Nathan took out his wallet and they settled up.

As the proprietor handed the large bag to Nathan, he said, "Tell your dad I said have a happy Thanksgiving."

"I'll do that."

As they stepped away from the stand, Sara said to Nathan, "I thought you didn't shop here."

"I don't, but Davidson supplies turkey products to the lodge. I'd forgotten he had a stand here, too, until you mentioned wanting to shop at a market."

As they strolled down the aisles, from food stand to

food stand, Nathan recognized many of the proprietors, and nodded and said hello. When they paused at a bakery to purchase fresh rolls and bread, the smiling, round-faced, white-haired woman looked up at Nathan and asked, "Can Kyle have a doughnut?"

When Nathan looked at his son to see if he wanted one, Kyle grinned and nodded.

A piece of wax paper in her hand, she picked out a freshly glazed doughnut and handed it to him. "Your daddy liked my doughnuts when he was a boy, too. That's when I took orders for them from my house," she explained to Sara. "Every Friday afternoon Galen picked them up on his way home from the textile mill."

"Why don't you give me a dozen of them," Nathan suggested. "Ben's flying in tonight. He could always eat four at a sitting."

"Your daddy always told me that the three of you boys squabbled over them, and he was lucky if he got *one*."

"I'll be sure to save him one," Nathan told her.

Kyle happily took another bite of his doughnut. Sara's elbow brushed Nathan's as they walked away. She felt the current to her eyebrows.

"I guess in a town this size, everyone knows everyone," she murmured.

"It seems that way sometimes."

After an awkward silence, she asked, "So your dad worked in a textile mill?"

"He was a foreman until it closed down. Then he got a job managing the hardware store."

"Until you opened the lodge?"

"It was his suggestion, actually. The place was for sale a long time, and nobody wanted to take it on. After Colleen—" Nathan stopped. "After I became a single parent, I didn't want to work the hours I was putting in as an analyst. So Dad suggested we buy the lodge, and it worked out well."

"Are you happy here?"

"As happy as I can be."

From the pictures of his wife in his house, Sara guessed Nathan still longed for the marriage he'd once had, longed for Colleen's presence here with Kyle, missed her and always would.

When Kyle asked his dad a question, Sara took the opportunity to walk ahead, to move away from Nathan's masculine presence, his deep voice, the furrow in his brow that she'd like to ease away. Instead of searching for more produce, she headed for an alcove with grapevine trellises on three sides, dried flower arrangements and colorful baskets. She was inside the booth, Kyle following her, when she heard Nathan practically shout, "No, Kyle, come here. You can't go in there."

Alarmed, and not knowing why Nathan had called to Kyle, she glanced over her shoulder and saw him take his son's hand and herd him in another direction.

She raced after them. "What's wrong?"

"The dried flowers, the potpourri, the scents. They could set him off. They'll cause an attack quicker than anything." Nathan sounded almost angry, and she realized she could have led Kyle into harm's way.

Kyle yanked on his dad's hand. "Sara didn't know, Daddy. Don't be mad at her."

Nathan hunkered down in front of him and dropped his bags to the floor. He took Kyle by the shoulders. "I'm not mad at her. I was concerned for you. You have to know to stay away from those things, too."

"I forget sometimes," Kyle responded.

"I know you do, especially if it's in a place where everything else is safe for you. But now you'll know when you smell something pretty and sweet, you should probably go in the other direction, okay?"

Kyle nodded and looked up at Sara. "Okay?"

She laid her hand on his head. "I got it. If anything smells sweet or strong, we should go in the other direction."

She tried to read Nathan's expression, but couldn't. However, she knew what he was thinking. He couldn't trust Kyle with her.

As soon as she had some spare time, she would research asthma on the Internet, learn about it and order a few books. More than anything, she didn't want Nathan to worry when Kyle was with her.

The boy kept up a constant chatter in the car as they drove back to the lodge. He'd been stimulated and excited about everything he'd seen and done, and it bubbled out. He was grown-up for a five-year-old, and Sara suspected his maturity stemmed from being around adults most of the time.

He helped them carry all the bags inside, like a little

trouper, lugging whatever he could. His green eyes sparkled when he said, "I can't wait till Uncle Ben gets here…till he sees we bought a real turkey."

"We've always had real turkey before," Nathan protested. "It was just already on the plate with mashed potatoes and gravy."

"But we never cooked one. Can I help you, Sara?"

Her gaze went to Nathan's. "You can help as long as you stay away from the oven when it's hot."

"But I can look in while it's cooking, can't I?" Kyle asked, still excited by the idea.

"I'll let your dad open the oven door so you can peek in. How's that?"

"Super. I'll draw a picture of the market so I can show Val," he said and was off to his room, leaving Sara and Nathan in the kitchen.

Sara stood to one side as Nathan slid the turkey into the refrigerator. Before he could close the door, she opened the crisper drawer and deposited the broccoli and other vegetables there. The awkwardness between them wasn't going to be dispelled easily, but she had to make a stab at it.

"I'm sorry about what happened at the market."

"You didn't know."

"Maybe we should have a discussion about asthma, and you could tell me everything I need to know."

"That's easier said than done. Most of what I've learned has been by experience. But I do have a folder of materials that the doctor gave me, if you're interested."

"I'm interested."

They gazed into each other's eyes for a very long time, as Sara's words seemed to echo with a double meaning. Flustered, she finally picked up the sack of potatoes. "Where should I put these?"

He took them from her. "Nowhere. We'll leave them on the counter. We're going to peel them tomorrow. Look, Sara, in spite of what happened, Kyle seemed to have a good time. When he was practically skipping through the market, I realized how limited his life has become."

"You've got the toughest job a parent can have, being protective, yet letting him find his own way."

"I've concentrated on being protective since he was three. It seemed the best way to be. But seeing him with you today…"

"I don't understand."

"He's different when he's with you, Sara. Maybe it's because you don't have a preconceived notion of what he can and can't do. That sets him free."

"I can't tell whether you think that's good or bad."

"It's neither. It just is. Truth be told, I'm a little jealous, I guess. He constantly looks to me for approval or direction. I don't think he sees me as a person he can have fun with." Nathan seemed unsettled by that.

"You can change that, you know."

"Can I? I'm not so sure. Being an effective parent, I don't know if I can be his friend, too."

"It might become easier as he gets older."

Nathan gave her a wry grin. "Somehow I doubt that."

"Are you and your brothers friends with your dad?"

For a moment, Nathan looked as though he didn't want to step into personal territory. But then he leaned against the counter and thought about it. "He's more parent than friend. With three of us, he had to have a strong hand. When he set up rules, we knew if we broke them, there would be consequences."

"It sounds as if he was a good role model."

"He was. Maybe a little uncommunicative at times, really removed after our mother left. Sam and Ben and I would get bent out of shape when he'd sit in his recliner for an hour, just staring into space, not saying a word."

"I imagine he had a lot to sort out. Was your mother's leaving…" Sara hesitated. "Unexpected?"

Again, Nathan seemed to be uncomfortable talking about it, but he answered her. "It was like a bomb exploded. Our world blew up, and we didn't really know what had happened. One day she was there, the next day she wasn't."

"Your dad didn't see it coming, either?"

"He rarely talks about it. From what he *has* said, I think she was dissatisfied, unhappy for a couple of years. But he didn't know what to do about it."

"How old were you when she left?"

"I was nine, Ben was six and Sam was three. Our mother was from Liverpool and earned her degree in English literature before she came here on a trip and met Dad. She found a job substitute teaching at the Rapid Creek high school and worked part-time at the feed store. The three of us came along pretty quickly. She left us when she was accepted into a doctorate program at Oxford. She hadn't even told Dad she'd applied. She just packed her bags, insisted it was his turn to take care of us, and flew away."

Nathan was telling the story somewhat dispassionately, but Sara sensed that underneath there was a strong current that still ran through his life—the angst of being abandoned by his mother. "Didn't she come back to see you?"

"She didn't come back period. It turns out she'd grown to hate Rapid Creek and its limitations. When she divorced Dad, she moved on. It was as if one day she was one person, and the next she was someone else. Or else she'd hidden who she was all along, and everything she was feeling. At least from us."

Sara was shaking her head. "I can't imagine it. I mean, I can understand problems between a husband and wife, but I can't imagine a mom leaving her kids." She was standing close to Nathan now. He was tall and muscled and full of strength, yet she wanted to put her arms around him. She wanted to console the boy he'd once been.

"Don't look so sad for us, Sara. It's over and done."

She wasn't so sure of that. The past had a way of digging its claws very deep. Sometimes the wounds didn't heal, and sometimes the scars never went away.

"I never knew my dad," she confided. "I mean, he and my mom didn't marry. When she found out she was pregnant, he took off. He had a life he wanted to live, and a baby didn't fit into it. My mother tried contacting him after I was born, through a buddy of his, but he simply didn't care."

"Did you search for him as an adult?"

"When my mom was diagnosed with her blood disorder, I think she felt as if she still had to take care of me. She gave me my father's social security number. An acquaintance from high school who'd become a policeman searched for an address and obtained one. Mom left messages and she wrote, but we never heard from him. I think it's obvious he just didn't want to be saddled with any responsibility. How about you? Do you know where your mother is now?"

"Before I went to college, I asked my dad if he knew where she was. I remember the expression on his face— part resentment, part bitterness, part sadness. He said she'd died five years before, from a skiing accident in the Alps. His name had been in her belongings. A friend of hers thought my dad would want to know. When I asked why he didn't tell us, he said it was because she was already dead to us. He didn't feel a need to bring it up. Sam was fifteen then, and when I told him, I think he was devastated. As the youngest, he'd always harbored the hope that she'd come back. Dad should have told us so that we could have faced reality."

"Maybe that reality was easier for your brother to face at age fifteen than it would have been earlier."

"I don't know. Sam's the optimist in the family. At least he was until…"

"Until?"

"Until he hooked up with the wrong woman. He won't be here for Thanksgiving because he's nursing wounds, trying to find himself again. If he doesn't do it soon, Ben and I might have to shake some sense into him."

Although she could hear frustration in Nathan's voice, she heard much more caring and affection and brotherly worry. "So the three of you are close?"

After thinking about that for a minute, he shrugged. "I guess you could say we are. We usually talk often. At least we did until this breakup of Sam's. He doesn't even have a phone at the cabin where he's staying, and there's no cell signal."

"You're really worried?"

"I'm really worried."

Nathan obviously wasn't going to say more on the subject. After all, it was private Barclay business, and she wasn't a Barclay.

Whenever Sara was this close to Nathan, she could breathe in his scent—fresh soap and male. His shoulders were broader than any man's she'd ever known. His gray eyes were intense. She wondered what he'd be like if he really let go and laughed, actually relaxed.

With his gaze on her, as if he was still trying to figure her out, he said, "Kyle's never had a real Thanksgiving dinner. We always brought it in from the lodge before. This could be a holiday he won't forget."

"Holidays should be memorable, don't you think? Each holiday should bring back good memories of family times and traditions. But you don't need a home-cooked turkey to make it one to remember, not if you're around people who love you. My mom and I spent most Thanksgivings alone. Everyone always seemed to have family to go to on Thanksgiving. We still had great memories, watching *Miracle on 34th Street,* and digging into whatever dessert she made, of going to church first thing in the morning to give thanks for what we had."

Sensing she'd already revealed too much, she changed the subject. "Speaking of dessert, what kind of pie do you like? I might make that tonight. I bought apples, or I can make chocolate cream."

"That's a tough decision." His smile was a little wry, but she could see amusement in his eyes. She suddenly wanted to make this holiday the best Thanksgiving the Barclays had ever had.

"How about one of each? With three grown men and a five-year-old, we're going to need two pies."

His smile faded. "Are you trying to prove something, Sara? Or maybe earn approval?"

She didn't look away, but answered as honestly as she could. "I don't think so. I can't just sit around like a house-guest. I'm a doer, Nathan, a type-A personality and all that. The truth is, I guess I wouldn't mind some approval from you rather than constantly getting the feeling you want to throw me out."

"I don't want to throw you out." His voice was husky, and she saw that it was hard for him to admit.

If she moved a step closer to him, would he come a step closer to her? She didn't have the courage to find out.

"Well, good," she said lightly. "Then all I need to know is whether or not your housekeeper has two pie plates in your cupboards." Taking a deep breath, she moved away from him, toward the table where groceries were scattered, and lifted the sack of flour.

When she wasn't with Kyle, she had to keep busy. And she had to stay away from Nathan. She had to remind herself he could kick her out whenever he wanted, and although he said he wouldn't, she knew if she became a threat to him, he wouldn't hesitate to put her out of his home…and out of Kyle's life.

After supper, Nathan found Sara in her bedroom, seated on the straight-back chair she'd pulled up to the table at the window. A laptop computer was open in front of her. The aroma of freshly baked pies hung in the air, giving his log home a warm ambience it didn't often have. Tonight was different from when Val prepared suppers and left them for him and Kyle.

Sara was engrossed in what she was reading on her screen, and Nathan wondered if she'd brought work along. That wouldn't be unusual, with the kind of hours she put in.

He rapped lightly on the door frame, entered and moved closer to her. As he did, he caught sight of the heading on the screen. She wasn't working. She was reading about asthma. This woman had a gung ho spirit about everything she did.

"This is complicated," she murmured as she looked up at him. "You never know what's going to happen next."

"It can be unpredictable," he agreed. "All I can do is take precautions and hope they work."

"Yes, I read that, but I also read that doctors believe that asthmatics can live normal lives now with new medications and therapies. That's the goal."

"I suppose everyone's interpretation of normal is different."

"I guess so."

"Reading about the condition is fine, Sara, but experiencing it is a whole other ball game."

Nodding, she pushed her chair away from the table and stood. They were in close proximity, the same kind they'd experienced that night in her kitchen, when neither of them had been wearing many clothes.

He noticed she'd tied her hair back in a ponytail while she'd been baking. She'd let Kyle handle the dough, too, and they'd both ended up with flour smears on their faces. She still had a bit of flour over her left cheekbone. Before Nathan could catch himself, he wiped it away with his thumb. Her skin was damnably soft, porcelain smooth, enticing. A rush of arousal swept through him, so fast he couldn't hold it at bay.

She stood perfectly still, just looking at him, not even blinking.

He fought for control over a base hunger he hadn't fed in years. "I'm picking up Ben at the airport. I wondered if you'd mind staying with Kyle. It's a cold night and I don't particularly want to take him out. I should be back in forty-five minutes, unless Ben's plane is late. If it is, I'll call you."

"I don't mind. I'm surprised you trust me with him."

"I know for sure he took his medication this morning. I saw him swallow it. Since his last attack, I think he understands the importance of not skipping a day, not brushing it aside because he doesn't feel like doing it. There are two inhalers on the counter in the kitchen. I've already shown you how to prepare them. Dad should be stopping by in a few minutes. He knows the drill, too."

"That's why you're going to let me sit with Kyle. You know I have backup."

"I didn't want you to be uneasy about it, either."

She didn't look as if she believed him.

"Sara…" How could he explain that too many precautions were never enough? How could he explain that he didn't want her to be Kyle's mother, but that he couldn't stop his heart from racing when he was around her? How could he dismiss the arousal that he hadn't experienced since before his wife had died? How could he ignore the pull of attraction that was drawing him closer to her?

"Sara," he said again, and slid his hand under her ponytail. Maybe if he kissed her and nothing happened, he could forget about all of this. If nothing happened, he could go back to wishing her out of his life.

But something *did* happen.

Shooting reason all to hell, canning the idea that nothing special was going on here, when his lips covered Sara's, he was young again, experiencing sexual arousal for the first time, acting on it as if he knew no boundaries, as if the moral code he lived by didn't exist. He forgot who he was and who she was, and where they were. All that mattered was the touch of his lips on hers and the sweep of his tongue into her mouth. He groaned with a pure erotic pleasure he hadn't felt for so very long. That pleasure came from her response, the immediate tightening of her hands on his shoulders, her tongue's play with his, a little sound she made in her throat. She was all tantalizing woman, as tempting as Eve.

Was her response genuine? Or was she playing a game, attempting to win him over, planning to eventually have some claim on Kyle?

Could she be that devious? He wasn't as cynical as Ben. Nathan had known the love of a faithful, devoted woman.

Colleen.

He broke away abruptly, haunted by guilt that he was somehow betraying his dead wife, suspicious that Sara could be playing him to gain more time with his son.

Taking a few steps back, he muttered, "I never should have done that."

She kept silent.

"You know as well as I do that more complications are only going to mess up our lives."

"They aren't in a mess yet," she said quietly.

"No, they're not, and we're going to keep it that way." He crossed to the door. "As I said, Dad will be here in about ten minutes. Ben is staying at Dad's suite in the lodge and will probably stop in to say hi to Kyle, and to meet you."

"I need to win Ben's approval, too?" she asked lightly.

"Ben doesn't approve of anyone easily. Don't expect too much from him, Sara. As an assistant district attorney, he sees the worst of life every day."

"I'll remember that."

As Nathan nodded and left her room, he wondered if she'd remember their kiss, too. It was going to take him a hell of a long time to forget it.

But forget it he would. He really had no choice.

Chapter Five

"I still can't believe you invited her to stay here with you. I can't believe you invited her to Rapid Creek at all!" Ben hiked his weekender suitcase higher on his shoulder over his leather jacket.

Nathan let out a sigh that made a huge puff of white in the harsh evening air. He'd waited until he and his brother had exchanged handshakes, claps on the back that were almost a hug, and half the ride to Pine Grove Lodge before he'd explained that Sara would be joining them for the holidays. With the stony calmness Nathan knew his brother exhibited in the courtroom, Ben had ticked off reason after reason why Nathan should send her back to Minneapolis as soon as possible. Although Nathan had listened, his silence had frustrated Ben.

Now at the entrance to his house, he wasn't going to argue about it. "You're not living this, Ben. It's not as simple as you think it is."

"I didn't say it was simple." His brother drove his fingers through his thick black hair. "But I don't want you or Kyle to get hurt, and you're asking for trouble with this arrangement."

"It's not an arrangement."

"It's going to get very sticky if she *is* his mother."

"That's what I have to settle. I can't live with this sword hanging over my head."

"It'll be more than a sword if she takes you to court. This whole egg-retrieval thing is very murky. Yes, she signed a release, but everything could depend on a judge. You should get yourself a lawyer as soon as you can."

"And who should I get? Mr. Murphy, who's been handling wills since Dad was a kid?"

"You need to find someone who specializes in custody law. If you want, I'll check around. But I mean it, Nathan, you need an expert, somebody good who can stop this thing before it gets started."

"I'll think about it. For now, I just need to know for sure if she *is* Kyle's mother."

"You should have left well enough alone."

"I couldn't."

Ben lifted his gaze to the starry night sky, as if praying for patience, and then shook his head. "You're as contrary as Sam."

"Not possible," Nathan concluded with a wry grin, and opened the door to his home.

They'd no sooner stepped into the house than Kyle came barreling toward Ben from where he'd been kneeling at the coffee table, playing dominoes with Sara and his grandfather.

"Uncle Ben, Uncle Ben! Dad said you were bringing me a surprise."

Somehow Ben managed to drop his suitcase and lift Kyle almost to the ceiling. A moment later he settled him on the floor once more. "What happens after I give you the surprise? Do you want me to leave?"

"No," Kyle practically shouted. "Sara's gonna cook a turkey. You can eat with us. Can you smell the pies?"

Nathan watched as Ben assessed the kitchen—pies cooling on the counter, bread pulled apart for stuffing, a roasting pan ready for turkey. Then he turned his attention to the living room, where Galen and Sara sat on the sofa. She straightened and squared her shoulders, tensing for this meeting. Their dad was slouched in the corner of the sofa, appearing as relaxed as ever.

"I hear you have a new friend," Ben said casually to Kyle. "Maybe you should introduce me to her."

Taking his uncle at his word, Kyle grabbed Ben's hand and dragged him over to the coffee table. "This is Uncle Ben, Sara. He was a kid when Dad was."

Nathan had to chuckle at that.

In his professional, polite manner, Ben extended his hand to Sara, and she shook it, saying, "It's good to meet you."

Ben gave a curt nod, as if they'd see about that, and pulled back his hand. "Nathan tells me you're a lawyer."

"I am, but I don't do anything as courageous as you do."

"Nathan explained you're a corporate lawyer. You look for loopholes and protection for your clients."

Instead of reacting with a defensive response, Sara replied calmly. "That's one way of looking at it, I suppose. Another is that I help a business grow in the best way possible, so it's an impetus in the community where it's located. What would our communities be without corporations and businesses that hire residents, so families can benefit, too?"

"Touché." Ben gave a quick tilt of his head, as if she'd won the point.

"Can I have my surprise now?" Kyle asked, pulling on his hand.

"Are you sure you don't want to wait until tomorrow?" Ben teased.

Kyle solemnly shook his head.

"Okay." He took something from his pocket and dropped down onto his haunches. "Hold out your hand."

When Kyle did, Ben placed a charcoal-colored arrowhead onto his palm.

"This one isn't even broken! Not even a little."

"That's why I thought you'd like it. You might want to take extra care with it, though, and keep it separate from all the broken ones."

When Ben straightened, Galen stood up, stepped around the coffee table and pulled his son, who was taller than he was, into a hug. "Good to see you, boy."

"You, too, Pop."

Ben's voice was husky, and Nathan knew sometimes his brother wished he hadn't left Rapid Creek. Yet Ben had always been on a crusade, intending to make the world safe for everyone. Rapid Creek didn't need him. Albuquerque did.

"Are you going to stay and play dominoes with us?" Kyle asked.

"It's your bedtime," Nathan reminded him. "You're going to have a big day tomorrow. You'll have all day to spend with Uncle Ben then."

"Your dad's right, sport." Ben ruffled Kyle's hair. "I'm pretty beat, too. I'm going over to Gramps to settle down for the night myself. But I'll be back tomorrow before that turkey's on the table."

"Everything should be ready about one," Sara interjected.

Ben gave her another assessing glance. "All right. I'll be over around eleven, if I won't be in anybody's way."

"Not in mine," she assured him. "I'll be in the kitchen."

"Sara said I can help," Kyle exclaimed.

"With what?" Ben asked.

"With stuffing the turkey, and washing the potatoes, and stirring stuff into the broccoli."

Ben raised his eyebrows at that.

"It's a casserole," Sara explained, but then turned to Kyle. "If you want to play with your uncle, that's fine. You can always help me cook another time."

Nathan could see that Sara would bend over backward

to make sure everything went smoothly. He was grateful for that. She didn't seem to be territorial at all where Kyle was concerned. But he wondered if she was putting on an act, if she was just waiting, as he was, to find out the truth. Then what would she do?

Five minutes later, after another hug from Kyle, and a thank-you for the arrowhead, Ben and Galen left.

"Put on your pajamas," Nathan directed the boy. "After you brush your teeth, I'll read you a story."

"Can Sara read one, too?"

"I suppose we'll have time for two. Get started."

As Kyle ran off, Sara stacked the dominoes into their box. "Your brother doesn't like me," she said in a low voice.

"My brother doesn't know you."

"Knowing me has nothing to do with it. He doesn't like the fact that I've unsettled your life. I understand that."

Crossing to the sofa, Nathan sat beside her. She wasn't looking at him, just stacking the dominoes. He took hold of her elbow. "Ben is Ben. He doesn't take anyone at face value."

"I wasn't just doling out idle flattery when I said it takes courage to be a district attorney."

"Ben's got plenty of courage, but sometimes he has tunnel vision. Too often he sees himself as that knight on the white charger. He can't handle it when he falls off."

That brought a smile to Sara's lips, and Nathan realized how much he liked it.

"He doesn't have anyone special he cares about?"

"He doesn't trust women. That's the crux of it."

"Because your mother left?"

"Dad thinks so. I'm not so sure. I'd bet another woman disappointed him along the way."

Both of them paused, gazing into one another's eyes, connecting again in that man-woman way that had led to their kiss. The stillness in the room was almost profound.

Sara murmured, "He sure loves Kyle, though. That's obvious."

"Yeah, he does. He cares about all of us."

"I've always wanted a brother or sister," she admitted softly. "Do you realize how lucky you are?"

Suddenly he did. He thought about Sara, all alone now with no relatives. His dad and brothers were part of the fabric of his life. If he ever needed anything, they'd be there.

"Dad, I'm ready," Kyle yelled from the bedroom.

"Go ahead," Sara told him. "I'll put these away."

She was trying hard not to steal his time with his son. Before the conversation they'd just had, Nathan had thought Sara was too ambitious to leave Minneapolis for a town like Rapid Creek. But if she was Kyle's mother, he was the only relative she had in this world.

Would she move here?

She was a fascinating woman, and Nathan was becoming more captivated by her day by day. That wasn't good. The sooner Ben found him the name of a good custody lawyer, the better.

* * *

Sara mixed mashed sweet potatoes with brown sugar and butter. "Sprinkle the crumbs on top." Kyle had already cut in the butter, and the topping was just the way it should be.

"You're doing a great job. You can help me in the kitchen anytime."

The boy beamed at her.

"What are you making?" Ben Barclay asked as he came up behind them.

"A sweet potato casserole," Kyle answered. "We're making it instead of candied sweet potatoes because I don't like candied sweet potatoes and Sara thought I'd like this."

"Can you check to see if I have enough hot plates on the table, honey? We need four."

When Kyle ran to the table, Ben commented, "You know how to pump up his self-worth."

"Isn't that what adults are supposed to do for kids?"

"I suppose. I get the feeling you think Nathan coddles him a little too much."

"Nathan's a good father."

"I don't see how you can decide that after a short visit."

"Mr. Barclay—"

"Call me Ben." He was smiling, but Sara knew it wasn't a real smile. It didn't make creases beside his eyes. It didn't give off any warmth.

Knowing she had to meet Nathan's brother head-on, she responded, "The first day I visited with Kyle, I could tell

Nathan was a good father. He's firm but not too stern. He gives lots of hugs and he cares about what Kyle says. It's easy to see that Nathan knows exactly *how* to be a father."

After a few moments, Ben admitted, "I guess you're more perceptive than I gave you credit for."

"You didn't give me any credit, Mr.—Ben. But that's fine. I don't have anything to prove—not to *you,* anyway."

He didn't look offended, but rather amused. "You tell it like it is, don't you?"

"This situation is too important to do otherwise."

"What do you ultimately want, Sara?"

What *did* she ultimately want? She wanted to be Kyle's mother, but she was beginning to want Nathan in her life as much as Kyle. She wanted to spend time with Kyle alone, but she doubted if Nathan would ever let her do that. Finally, she answered, "I want what's best for Kyle."

"Even if that's not best for you?"

"Even if. I know what you probably think, Mr. Barclay." She didn't correct herself this time. "You think I came for more money or a stake in someone else's family that will make mine better. But you're wrong about all that. I have a life in Minneapolis. I have a job that someday could make me very well off. I have ambitions and persistence, and the means to make it happen. I also know I can tell you all this until I'm blue in the face, and it won't make a difference, because you're going to think what you want to think."

"You're one tough cookie, aren't you?"

She wasn't sure whether she heard respect in his voice

or not. "I'm a lawyer, like you. I ask questions. I have to find the answers or I don't sleep at night."

"And just what are those questions, Sara?" Nathan's brother's voice was deceptively gentle.

"There's only one *important* question. Will my being in Kyle's life make it better? That's the only one I'm interested in answering right now."

Ben was studying her as if he were trying to find the truth. She'd given it to him, and if he couldn't accept it, that was just too bad.

"When we were younger," Ben said in a conversational tone, "Nathan took care of me and Sam. He felt that was his responsibility as the oldest. Now, things have evened up a bit. Now I watch out for him, too, as well as everyone else in my family."

"You're all lucky to have each other." Awkwardness grew between them until she murmured, "If you'll excuse me, I need to baste a bird."

Once Galen arrived, the men watched sports on TV, played board games with Kyle and spoke about people Sara didn't know. For the most part, their bonding consisted of laughter and activity rather than talking. When she wasn't busy in the kitchen, she observed them with interest. She'd never had quite this close a look into a family before. The longing that overtook her to be a part of that family startled her, mainly because she didn't understand it. She'd always been independent, always stood up for herself, and for the past few years depended on no one else. So why did she feel so drawn to the Barclay circle?

When the timer on the stove buzzed, indicating that the turkey was finished cooking, she opened the oven door, pulled it out and smiled. It was golden-brown and the legs were practically falling off. Before she could slip on the oven mitts, Nathan was there. Maybe he'd been watching her while she'd been watching him?

"I can get that." He used the mitts himself and hoisted the bird out of the oven to the top of the stove. They were standing elbow to elbow, and she remembered everything about his kiss, everything about his arms holding her, everything about his taste and smell. The silver sparks in his gray eyes had her wondering if he was remembering, too.

Gruffly, he asked, "Where do you want it?"

"Let me scoop out the dressing and then we can carve it on the table, if that's okay with you."

"That's fine."

He looked around the kitchen, at the sweet potato casserole on the rack on the counter, the broccoli-and-almond casserole in another serving dish, the salad and cranberry sauce and gravy she'd already prepared. "You really went all out."

"It's Thanksgiving."

For an instant, just an instant, his face gentled and all the remoteness was gone. Just as quickly it was back. "Let's scoop out that stuffing so everything doesn't get cold."

Sitting around the table a few minutes later, all except

Nathan, who stood with a carving knife above the turkey, Sara asked, "Can we give thanks?"

The brothers exchanged looks.

Galen answered, "Sure we can."

"I thought maybe instead of just saying a prayer, we could each mention something we're thankful for."

The men seemed uncomfortable with that.

"Just one-liners, nothing elaborate. I think it makes our thanks more real."

Galen sat up straight and nodded. "I think it's a fine idea. Why don't you go first, Sara?"

"I want to give thanks for Nathan inviting me into his home for Thanksgiving." She nodded to Galen.

"I want to thank the Lord for another successful year at the inn. We're booked up clear to spring. Thank you, thank you."

Ben was next. He looked totally stumped for a few moments, then gave a half smile. "I want to give thanks for that arrowhead I found for Kyle to add to his collection."

Nathan put his arm around his son. "I'll give thanks that Kyle is happy and healthy today."

There was silence as everyone looked at Kyle. He shifted a moment in his chair, as if he wasn't exactly sure what he wanted to say, but then he smiled. "I want to give thanks for Sara."

The table was quiet until Nathan stepped into the gap. "And for all the wonderful food she made for us. This will be a Thanksgiving to remember."

She didn't hear regret in Nathan's voice, or sarcasm. He seemed to be just making a statement. But she was sure his mind was filled with the Thanksgivings he'd shared with Colleen, and how different life would be now if she had lived. As if to reinforce her thought, his gaze shifted quickly to a photograph of his wife on the sideboard, then returned to the turkey he was going to carve. In that moment, Sara knew Nathan had loved deeply. He wasn't the type of man to forget his marriage, or the woman he'd chosen to spend the rest of his life with.

Fortunately, Galen passed her the broccoli and asked where she'd learned to cook so well. She tried to put Nathan and Colleen and their marriage out of her mind, and just concentrate on the here and now…concentrate on having Thanksgiving with Kyle.

After all the food had been passed around and everyone was enjoying it, Kyle said, "I wish Uncle Sam could be here. When's he coming home?"

Nathan and Ben exchanged knowing looks. Nathan put his arm around Kyle's shoulders. "We don't know, but soon, we hope."

"He'd be here," Galen muttered, "if that fiancée of his hadn't gone and had an abortion…."

"Dad," Nathan warned.

Galen looked at Kyle. "Right."

But Kyle was busy digging into his sweet potatoes, and appeared not to have heard his grandfather.

"That's what happened?" Sara asked Galen. "Is that why he went away?"

"He had a real tough time accepting what she did. He and Alicia had plans to build a house. But that fell flat when he learned what she'd done." Galen kept his voice low. "Sam has a heart of gold. That woman broke it. I know he was dreaming about having a mess of kids."

"When did they break up?" Sara kept her own voice a murmur. Nathan and Ben were engrossed in a conversation of their own.

"In August, Sam broke it off. He said he could never forgive her...never trust her again."

"Once trust is broken it's difficult to fix."

"I kept quiet when he got engaged, but I never thought Alicia was right for him. Too flighty, too selfish. I think it's better he found out now rather than later. Maybe during this time alone in those woods he'll figure out what he wants next."

From what Kyle had told her about Sam, the games they played together and his dog Patches, the youngest Barclay sounded more playful and freer than either Ben or Nathan. Sara hoped she'd have a chance to meet him someday.

The house was quiet now as Nathan headed for the pie dish and the last piece of apple pie. Earlier in the evening Kyle had asked if Sara would read him a story and say bedtime prayers with him. What could Nathan say? It was Thanksgiving. Sara had cooked a wonderful meal and he couldn't deny his son the attention he needed.

Nathan had come in on the tail end of those prayers, and

had seen the hug Kyle had given Sara. They were bonding and there was nothing he could do about it.

Other than send her packing.

When he heard Sara's loafers on the kitchen floor, he didn't turn around. "Do you want to toss a coin for the last piece of apple pie?"

"No thanks. I'm going to make a cup of tea. I bought chamomile at the market. Maybe it will help me sleep."

That brought his gaze to hers. The impact of looking into her green, green eyes always rocked him a little. "Are you jittery about the DNA test tomorrow?"

Breaking eye contact, she added water to the copper kettle from the tap. "Not so much. I'm more jittery about today." Her quick glance at him told him she wanted him to follow up on that comment.

He obliged. "Why?"

"Because I sense that you're angry that I changed the way you usually do things. That my being here has changed everything."

Was it the lawyer in her that was so perceptive, or the woman? Nathan ran his hand across his forehead. "Actually, I don't think you're sorry you *are* interfering. I think it's what you meant to do. You want to be a mother. You'd like to be part of Kyle's life. That's what today was all about. If you sense any anger from me, it's because I see what's happening and I know I have to protect Kyle."

"What are you protecting him from? Me? Getting hurt? If I *am* Kyle's mother, I'm going to want to spend more time with him. Then what are we going to do?"

"You said you'd go back to Minneapolis."

"I did. And I will. But I'll at least want to visit. I want Kyle to know who I am. How will you handle that? Will you try to shut me out of his life, or will you include me in it?"

The more Nathan studied Sara's features, the more he saw Kyle's. "I don't have the answer, Sara, not now, not yet. We have tomorrow to get through, and then a couple of weeks of waiting. There's no point jumping ahead of ourselves. We'll fall flat on our faces if we do."

"I like to know where my life is going and what I can expect next."

He recognized that desire. Ben was the same way. "That's the lawyer in you. There's no way to plan for the unexpected and you know it."

He saw how the uncertainty of the entire situation was shaking her and her world. There was nothing he could do about that. He just hoped it didn't shake his, too.

Chapter Six

"Tell me again why Miss Marie put that thing in my mouth. It felt funny."

Sara gazed down at Kyle and decided to let Nathan answer. After all, she wouldn't want to say the wrong thing. She wouldn't want to *do* the wrong thing. She was so afraid Nathan would toss her out of Kyle's life after the slightest bungling on her part.

As they headed toward Nathan's SUV in the parking lot of the medical center, he stopped to put his hand on his son's shoulder. "It's just a test we all decided to have done."

"What kind of test? I didn't have to answer questions."

Nathan's lips formed a smile for his son, but Sara could

see he wasn't smiling inside. "Not that kind of test. This one shows us something different. When we get the results, I'll tell you about it."

"But why can't I—"

Sara hunkered down beside Kyle. "Do you know what I heard? I heard that a crew put up Christmas decorations in the square. There's a tree, and a Santa Claus with a sleigh, and even pretend reindeer. Maybe your dad will swing by and we can see them."

"Pretend reindeer as big as real ones?" Kyle's tone of voice suggested that if they weren't that big they weren't worth going to see.

"I haven't seen them myself so I don't know for sure. I've also heard there's a special mailbox. You can write a letter to Santa, drop it in there and he'll get it."

"Really? Can we do that?"

"Sure we can. As soon as we get home…I mean back to your house."

"Home" had just slipped out. Nathan's house was a place where family gathered, where he and Kyle lived, where they roughhoused with his brothers. It was a home in every sense of the word. But also in that home, pictures of Colleen sat in almost every room. When the DNA results came back, could Nathan be honest with Kyle about them?

When she straightened and stood, Nathan clasped her shoulder. Kyle was already three steps ahead of them, walking toward the SUV. He now had a lot on his agenda and had forgotten all about the cheek swab in the doctor's office.

"Thank you."

Sara could see Nathan meant it. "Distractions go a long way with five-year-olds."

Noting the gratitude in Nathan's eyes, aware of his large, strong hand on her shoulder, she felt an odd rightness about both.

But then he pulled his hand away and the smile faded. "It's a shame adults can't be distracted as easily." A moment later he pressed the button to unlock the doors on the SUV.

Sara headed to the passenger's side, knowing that any rightness she felt was one-sided.

Later that afternoon at the lodge, Galen handed Nathan the list of supplies he needed for the following week. "What's that scowl for?" his father asked.

"I wish you'd just sit down at the computer at the lodge or the one in my bedroom and put the numbers in there. It would be so much easier."

"And ruin my eyes? No. I'll let you take care of that. I'd push the wrong button and you'd have to do it over, anyway."

"That's just an excuse," Nathan grumbled.

"When did you get that stone in your boot?"

"What stone?"

"The one that's making you grouchy."

Nathan sighed. "Kyle's writing a letter to Santa Claus, and he wanted *Sara* to help him instead of me."

"I see." His father just stood there, studying him.

"What do you see?"

"I see that you want things the way they were before."

"Of course I do. If she *is* his mother—"

Nathan didn't get a chance to finish. The door to the lodge opened, then Kyle burst inside ahead of Sara. "I'm all finished. And I didn't just ask for presents for me. I asked for presents for you and Uncle Ben and Uncle Sam, and even you, Gramps."

"Do I dare ask what you ordered for me?" Galen said with an amused expression.

"Sure. I told him you needed a new toolbox. Your old one's all rusty and the lid creaks and it won't close right." Kyle looked up at his dad. "I told Santa about those binoculars you want with the camera inside."

"They *would* be a very nice Christmas present. But they might be a little too expensive for Santa to bring."

"Santa can bring *anything*. I told him about the bracelet Sara liked in that magazine, too."

"But what did you tell Santa *you* want?" Galen asked with a laugh.

"I told him lots of stuff. I want a new fire engine, Power Rangers figures, books…and I want Uncle Sam to come home."

Nathan hunkered down next to his son. "You know Santa can't bring everything on your list. He has a lot of children to think about. And as far as Uncle Sam goes, Santa can't make decisions for him."

"No, but Sara said we would write down what I wanted, and that's something I wanted."

He'd have to have a talk with Sara and find out exactly what else Kyle had put in that letter. These days children didn't believe in Santa very long. Nathan wanted to uphold the myth for at least another year.

"I was going to go out back and fill the bird feeders," he said to Sara. "Would you like to come along?"

"Can I come, too?" Kyle asked.

"It's cold out there today."

"I could use your help sorting through the Christmas ornaments to put on the lodge tree. Think you can help me?" Galen asked the boy.

Kyle seemed torn for a moment, then broke into a smile. "Sure. And you can tell me a story about each one."

"If I did that, we'd never get them on the tree. Come on. Let's go to the storeroom and find the boxes."

"You want to know what was in Kyle's letter," Sara guessed, after Galen and Kyle had left the lobby area.

"I sure do. If I'm going to be Santa, I need an inside track."

She laughed, and Nathan realized again how much he liked the sound.

"Are you really going to fill the bird feeders? Or was that just an excuse to talk to me alone?"

"I'm really going to fill them, and you're welcome to join me. But you'll need your scarf and gloves and hat, maybe an extra pair of socks, too."

"I'll go to the house and get them. Where should I meet you?"

In spite of himself, Nathan felt a flicker of excitement

at the idea of rendezvousing with Sara. How crazy was that? It wasn't as if they were going on a date or anything. Dating a woman hadn't even occurred to him since Colleen had died. Why he was thinking of it now…

"Meet me at the kids' play area at the back of the lodge. And you don't have to hurry. It will take me a few minutes to gather the supplies we need."

"It won't take me long." With a smile and a wave, Sara left, and to Nathan's surprise, he felt her absence immediately. Energy she brought with her when she entered a room seemed to pulse all around her. He missed it when she was gone. Damn, what was wrong with him today?

To Nathan's surprise, she was waiting for him as he pushed the wheelbarrow down the back path. Colleen had always kept him waiting. She was never on time.

Sara peered into the wheelbarrow. "So you don't just pour birdseed into a feeder?" She picked up a wreath made up of all the seed any bird might like, then a similar triangle.

"We feed different types of birds. They like variety, too."

"Too?"

"Don't you like variety? In your day-to-day routine? In your food? In what you wear?"

As she thought about it, a tiny line creased her brow below her knit cap. "I guess I do. Although work is usually regimented, I enjoy getting a new case, the adrenaline rush of all the prep work."

"The tedium of the research?"

"How did you know?"

"Remember, Ben's a lawyer." Galen had taken him to the airport this morning. Ben had booked a seat on the first flight out. He never took much time off from work. Nathan knew he was dedicated, but also suspected Ben didn't have anything else to enrich his life.

Nathan and Sara filled a few wooden feeders hanging on the trees, and one freestanding one along the path, which looked like a pagoda.

As he hung the wreath on the highest branch he could reach on a tall oak, he asked, "So what else was in Kyle's letter?"

"A baseball mitt and bat, a model airplane kit, the Disney movie about the huskies, baseball cards, and a remote controlled Power Rangers motorcycle."

"You paid attention."

"I sure did. You'll have to tell me what you and Galen *aren't* going to get him, so there's something left for me."

"I think there's plenty to go around. I was debating about buying him one of those minicomputers for kids. It might help keep him occupied when he's bored, or when he wants to go outside and can't."

Nathan took a vertical-shaped bird feeder from the wheelbarrow. The different colors of the birdseed attached to it made it look festive. Adjusting the wire hanger, he slipped it around the branch and fastened it securely.

Sara came a little closer to examine it. Her breath puffed white as she traced her finger around the edge. She looked different today, with her knit cap pulled down on her head, her scarf wrapped around her neck, her cheeks already getting rosy from the cold. Usually she seemed so sophisticated, so much the professional, so polished. But today she could have been a girl who had grown up in Rapid Creek, who was used to snow and snowshoes and hiking around the paths at the lodge. One thing he'd noticed about Sara was that she seemed to be able to adapt to almost any situation. He didn't know if that was good or bad. He didn't want her to enjoy being in Rapid Creek, did he? Didn't want her to feel at home…

He watched her gloved index finger trace the design on the feeder, and he suddenly yearned to feel that finger on his skin. On his face. On his body.

Sara Hobart was a fascinating package.

"I've read the information in the folder you gave me. I've also been doing more research on asthma on the Internet." She was looking up at him, her eyes wide and clear.

"And?" he questioned.

"I never realized it was so complicated, or common. But stress is a component, just as in any disease. I can see why you'd want to protect a child with asthma, yet by doing so a parent could isolate him or her. And that wouldn't be good, either."

"Do you think I'm too protective of Kyle?"

"I think caring for and disciplining a child with asthma makes parenting even tougher. You do a great job."

"You didn't answer my question."

"It doesn't matter what I think, does it? You're going to do what you believe is best."

"Just like a lawyer. I can't get a straight answer."

He stooped to pick up the wheelbarrow's handles, ready to push it to the next stand of trees. But Sara caught his arm—the contact, even through his coat, tightened his gut.

She was close…close enough that her breath could mingle with his. "I think sometimes you *are* too protective. But then I haven't had to watch Kyle go through an attack. I haven't had to rush him to the hospital. I haven't had to stand by while he struggled for breath. So what I see might not be the real picture."

There was compassion in her eyes, and a willingness to understand that he found seductive.

The silence on this cold winter day was profound. In it they were a man and a woman, devoid of pretense, without defenses. The cold seemed to purify any contentiousness between them, seemed to draw them together so they could combine their warmth. At least that's what Nathan told himself as he leaned closer to Sara. As she leaned closer to him. The blue sky and the sun, hidden behind the clouds, seemed hushed and waiting.

Nathan knew that if he kissed Sara he'd feel alive again. That his body would find a little of the satisfaction it had been longing for. Yet if he kissed Sara…

All that mattered was this moment in time, which if it passed could never be recaptured. He bent his head, and when his lips touched hers, his arms went around her. His reactions were reflexive, male, natural. He didn't wait for an invitation. When he slid his tongue into her mouth, he breathed in the scent of her shampoo, mixed with pine, winter and desire. He'd never thought of desire as tangible before. But it was living and pulsing in the air, and in his body. It was all around him, taking over the kiss.

His hands played up and down her back, trying to feel her warmth under her jacket. When he slipped them under her hair, he was rewarded by the heat of her neck. The tiny sounds she made had him slipping one of his legs between hers, inching her back against the birch. They were anchored then. Her body was soft against his hardness. Her arms were eager as they held him close. Then the kiss exploded, their tongues dancing against each other, their mouths angling for better access, their breathing ragged as they took as much as they could out there in the cold yard with the possibility of guests roaming about.

This time Sara was the one who suddenly stopped, who pulled away, who looked at him in disappointment.

Somehow, he calmed his body's raging response, the racing beat of his heart, to ask, "What's wrong?"

"We shouldn't complicate an already complicated situation."

"That kiss wasn't about a situation. It was about a man and woman needing each other." He could hear the strain in his voice, and knew what he said was true. His body needed Sara's. No woman had made him want like this since Colleen had died.

"How can we get involved, when you could shut me out

of your life? Out of Kyle's life? I realize why you want to do that. You want Kyle to remember Colleen as his mother. I think you still love her. There's nothing I can do about that."

Sara's words hit Nathan like a belly blow. Sure, he still loved Colleen. She'd been his wife. They'd had Kyle and Mark together. He'd been faithful to her, and had expected to go fishing with her in their old age. Of course he still loved her.

Whatever Sara saw in Nathan's face galvanized her. Her expression was no longer open and her eyes became guarded. She slipped away from him, and the tree, and started for the house.

"Sara, wait."

But she didn't wait. She just kept walking. Nathan didn't call for her again. What was the point?

She was right.

"She thinks she's a mother just because she donated her eggs?"

Sara came around the corner into the kitchen and heard the older woman's hushed voice as she spoke to Nathan. Although Sara thought about retreating, she didn't.

It was the Monday after Thanksgiving, and Nathan's housekeeper, Val Lindstrom, was back. It was clear Sara and she would have to come to terms if they were going to spend time in the same house. Sara wasn't sure it was hostility she heard in the housekeeper's voice, but rather concern. She understood that.

Nathan looked uneasy as he spotted Sara.

She said politely, "Kyle's brushing his teeth and then he's going to get dressed. He wants me to read to him, and I thought maybe I'd play word games with him, if that's okay with you."

Val gave Nathan a hard look, and he said, "That's fine. Sara, this is Val Lindstrom. I don't know what I'd do without her."

Stepping forward, Sara extended her hand.

Val stared at it, took it and gave it a quick shake. "Nathan tells me you're staying the next couple of weeks." The woman wore her hair pulled back into a tight bun. It was mostly gray, with some brown streaks. Her words were as severe as her hairdo.

"Until the results of the DNA tests are in," Sara replied bluntly.

"What are you going to do if they come back saying you're Kyle's mother, biologically speaking?" Val asked, just as bluntly.

Sara wasn't put off by the housekeeper. She knew the older woman was concerned about Kyle and Nathan, and she'd just as soon have all their cards on the table. "If the results show that I'm Kyle's mother, I'll stay through the holidays. And as I told Nathan, if at any time my presence here is too much trouble, I can move into town."

"If you *are* Kyle's mom, you're just going to leave after that?"

"My job is in Minneapolis." That was supposed to say it all, but it didn't. If Kyle was her son, Sara was beginning to believe she would do anything for him, maybe even moving her life. Maybe even giving up the career she'd worked so hard for. She wasn't sure yet.

"I've got to get over to the lodge," Nathan said. "I told Dad I'd cover checkout for the guests this morning." He looked from one woman to the other. "Is everything going to be all right here?"

"Fine," both she and Val said at the same time.

Nathan's brows arched, and with a shake of his head he took his jacket from a hook at the door. "If I get tied up, don't hold lunch."

His last glance at Sara told her he was remembering their kiss. He'd kept superbusy over the weekend, as if he was trying to forget it. She had gone on lots of long walks, giving him time alone with his son, thinking, wondering if the results of the DNA test were going to change her life…all of their lives.

They'd gone to church together yesterday morning, and as she and Nathan had raised their voices in song, she'd felt such a rightness in being there beside him. She told herself she was just feeling that because of the bond she was forming with Kyle. The truth was, she was falling for Nathan Barclay, and she was going to get hurt. He wasn't free. He still loved his wife. He might make room in his life for Sara to visit Kyle. He might act on sexual urges that drove any man. But she wasn't going to delude herself into thinking he could feel more than that for her.

When Kyle came running into the room, he glanced at Sara and told her, "I brushed my teeth really good," then went to give Val a hug. She'd opened her arms to him and he held on tight. "I missed you. Sara made a turkey and let me help. And Uncle Ben was here and everything."

Val smiled down at him. "You can tell me all about it over breakfast. Scrambled eggs this morning, or pancakes?"

He screwed up his nose and then decided, "Pancakes. Can Sara help make the faces?"

"He likes to make faces with blueberries," Val explained. She gave him another squeeze and patted him on the head. "Sure, she can help."

During the making of breakfast, Sara felt Val's gaze on her often. She felt as if she was on probation and had to pass a test. The problem was, she didn't know the rules or requirements in order to pass. She tried to be as natural as she could, and tried to make conversation.

"Did you have a nice Thanksgiving?" she asked the housekeeper as the pancakes on the griddle began to form little bubbles around the edges.

"Fine."

"Nathan said you were spending it with your sister. Does she live far away?"

"About twenty miles. Kyle, we're ready for those blueberries."

Scrambling up on the chair beside Val, Kyle took them from the dish and dropped them onto the pancakes in the semblance of faces.

After he hopped down and Val concentrated on flipping the pancakes, Sara tried again. "Will you be taking time off over Christmas?"

Val planted her hands on her hips, the pancake turner

still in her hand. "Look, if you don't want me to be around while you're here—"

Glancing at Kyle, who was heading for his fire engine in the living room, Sara said quickly, "Please don't take offense. I don't want that at all. I'm just trying to make conversation."

Val gave a humph, then turned back to the pancakes. But Sara was determined to hold her ground and eventually communicate with this woman who was important to Nathan and Kyle.

She slid the carton of orange juice from the refrigerator and poured it into three glasses. "At church yesterday," Sara began, "I heard some women talking about a tree lighting ceremony tonight."

"If you're thinking of going, you'll probably have to go alone. Nathan doesn't like to take Kyle out into the cold at night. It can kick up his asthma."

"What does Kyle's doctor say about that?" Sara asked.

Val shoved the pancakes onto a plate. "You'll have to ask Nathan. I just know that Kyle's last attack scared him to death, and he's not taking any chances."

"He's not always going to be able to protect Kyle like this."

"I think in his head he knows that. But he loves that boy so much he'd put him in a protective bubble if he could, and stay there with him." Then, looking as if she'd said too much, Val called to Kyle. "Time for breakfast."

Neither Nathan nor Val wanted Sara to interfere in Kyle's life. But if she *was* his mother…

One decision at a time, she told herself. One decision at a time.

* * *

"Are you sure your brother won't mind?" Sara asked, as Nathan preceded her and Kyle up the stairs at the back of the clinic that led to Sam Barclay's apartment.

They'd compromised.

At first, when Sara had brought up the idea of going to the Christmas tree lighting ceremony, Nathan had said no. But when she'd pushed harder, asking if they couldn't bundle Kyle up, or put him in the car with the heater on, Nathan had given her a thoughtful look, then said he had an idea. From his brother's apartment, they could see the tree lighting ceremony. Having their own celebration, in Sam's warm living quarters above the veterinary clinic, they might even hear the carolers around the tree.

Sara knew watching from a distance wasn't the same as being there, but Nathan's idea was better than not going at all.

Excitedly, Kyle answered her question. "Uncle Sam won't mind. He said I can come stay with him anytime I want. Dad lets me sometimes, too."

"Sam knows the score," Nathan said, at her surprised look. "Kyle didn't test positive for allergies to dogs or cats. He can be around Sam's dog, Patches, without any problem."

"I love Patches. And so does Uncle Sam. He says Patches is his best friend."

Nathan opened the door and the three of them stepped inside. Sara could see it was definitely a bachelor pad, from the worn, gray corduroy sofa to the comfortable looking green recliner. A braided rug of gray, green, tan and bits of red warmed up the plank flooring. Although the furniture wasn't new, the entertainment unit certainly was.

Nathan's smile was rueful. "Sam likes to sit in the middle of his football games. That's a high definition TV. It almost gives a 3D effect."

Kyle was already at the front window, trying to get a look at the festivities. "Everyone's walking to the park," he announced. Then he ran to the side window, where he could see the tree itself. "Come on, Dad. Come on, Sara. I bet they're going to light the tree any minute."

Nathan checked his watch. "Fifteen minutes, cowboy. We have time to make hot chocolate first."

"Do you know where your brother keeps everything?" Sara asked with a smile.

"Sam's not complicated when it comes to that. He doesn't have a whole lot of pots and pans. But he likes chocolate, and keeps a supply of the instant mix on hand."

Nathan found a saucepan in a lower cupboard. "We can make one big batch instead of warming up each mug in the microwave."

When he turned on the faucet to fill the pan, Sara noted the serious expression on his face. "You're worried about your brother, aren't you?"

"It's really not like him to go off on his own. He's a social person, much more so than Ben or me. He likes groups of people. He can talk to anybody. But he's been so quiet the past few months. And now, leaving like this… Yeah, I'm worried."

"He might just need time to let the hurt diminish a bit. I know it's not the same thing, but after my mother died I really didn't want to talk to anyone for weeks."

Nathan seemed to think about that. "I didn't have that luxury after Colleen died. I had Kyle and a life with him to build. At work I was on the phone more than I was off of it. But I went through each day on automatic, so I guess you're right. Maybe Sam does need time alone to think."

The water started to boil. Sara handed Nathan the chocolate mix and he stirred it in. Their elbows brushed. Their gazes met. That electricity that had drawn them together in the backyard of the lodge was sparking and crackling. Sara's heart seemed to skip a beat, and she wished she knew what was going through Nathan's mind. She'd made the right decision pulling away from him, hadn't she?

But pulling away from Nathan just didn't seem right. Pulling away from him stirred up a loneliness she'd known for far too long.

"Someone's talking down there now," Kyle called to them.

"Probably the mayor," Nathan explained. "It'll be another five minutes, at least. We'll have time to drink our hot chocolate."

"Can we sing a Christmas carol when the tree gets lit up?" Kyle's face was so hopeful and so little-boy-Christmas wonderful that Sara saw Nathan smile ruefully. "Which one would you like to sing?"

"'Jingle Bells.' I know the words."

Kyle's mug was only half-filled and Sara helped him

with it so he didn't spill it. She also made sure he didn't burn himself. They had all taken a few sips when the tree lit up in all its splendor, a star twinkling on the top.

"Oh, look!" Kyle's voice was filled with awe.

Tears came to Sara's eyes…because it was Christmas and she cared about Kyle. Because it was Christmas and she was falling for Nathan.

"Who's going to start?" Nathan nudged his son.

"Let's start together. I'll count to three." Kyle lifted his hand and put down a finger with each number. "One, two, three."

They started singing, "'Dashing through the snow.'" After two verses, Kyle turned back to the window.

Sara put her arm around his shoulders, feeling Nathan's eyes on her. She knew he was asking himself what he was going to do if she *was* Kyle's mother.

Tonight she didn't need to know the answer to that question. Tonight she was satisfied just to be here like this.

Chapter Seven

Nathan didn't come to the cemetery often. He didn't even know why he'd had Colleen and the baby flown here to Rapid Creek after they died, because he'd still been living and working in Minneapolis. But in his grief and loss, he'd brought them to his hometown. Because that's where his family was? And that's where comfort lay?

There hadn't been any comfort.

The cemetery was still. Snow was falling. Anyone in his right mind wouldn't be out here now. Nathan was trying to *find* his right mind.

Peering down at his deceased wife's tombstone and the miniature one next to it, he felt…the hole. The hole they'd both left in his heart. The loss would always be with him, and he would always miss them. But the grief…the grief had changed. It was still there, but definitely not as intense. It was still there, yet sometimes he forgot about Colleen. And since he'd met Sara, sometimes he couldn't find the grief.

That worried him almost as much as feeling it all the time. He'd sensed a shift in his world's axis. That shift unsettled him. It disturbed him. Sara disturbed him.

Why had she awakened a sex drive that had been asleep for years? Why did his body respond to hers as if…as if it wanted to know hers so much better? As if a coupling could chase away any remnants of his grief. As if a tumble in bed was the only thing on his mind three-quarters of the day.

Not the only thing. Kyle was on his mind twenty-five hours a day. Kyle and the fact that if Sara *was* his mother she *could* have rights. Those rights might infringe on his.

He knew nothing good could come out of her being here. His logic told him if that DNA test was positive, he was in for a heap of trouble. Yet his body seemed to have a mind of its own where she was concerned.

If they got involved, would that make dealing with Kyle's situation better or worse?

He thought about the hot chocolate, and the lighting of the Christmas tree, and the Christmas carol they'd sung together. Anyone looking in, anyone hearing them, would think they were a family. It hurt. It hurt damn bad, thinking about the possibility that Kyle would know another woman as his mother. Yet didn't Kyle deserve to have a living mother? Didn't he himself deserve to have a woman warm his bed?

Not a woman who could take your son away, the wise voice inside of him warned.

Snow coated the top of the rose-granite, heart-shaped tombstone and Nathan felt colder than he could ever remember feeling. He longed to hear Colleen's voice, feel her presence, be sure she was watching over his son. Their son. But there was no message from above. No tap on his shoulder that told him everything would be all right. He could hardly even remember the sound of her voice.

When Nathan left the two graves, his heart was heavy from all he'd lost. After he made the trek to his SUV, snow collecting on his shoulders, he climbed inside and looked back at the two granite hearts.

Then he headed for home.

"I like the stars the best," Kyle announced as he painted one of the home-baked cookies with blue icing, then stuck a finger into the sweet goo and thrust it into his mouth.

Sara laughed when icing dribbled down his chin. "I think you like them *all* best."

They'd been baking cookies throughout the morning, and Kyle hadn't seemed bored with any of it. Val had been cleaning the house, stopping every once in a while to watch them or to listen to what they were saying.

Now she put down her feather duster on the counter and crossed over to Kyle. "I don't know why I never thought of making these kinds of cookies with you." She gazed at the racks of golden-brown cookies, some iced, some not, on the counter.

"Do you bake cookies at Christmas?" Sara asked conversationally.

"Galen's partial to chocolate chip, so I usually make those. He likes anything with lots of sugar and butter."

Sara remembered the way Nathan's dad had eaten at Thanksgiving. He was a big man and enjoyed his food. "He does a lot of hiking, doesn't he? He seems very fit."

"Oh, he's probably as fit as Nathan. But being fit and watching cholesterol isn't the same thing. I tell him if he isn't careful—" She broke off as if she thought she'd said too much.

"Are you and Galen friends?" Sara asked, not knowing whether or not the housekeeper might be offended by the question.

Val frowned. "We talk now and then. But he's always busy at the lodge, and…well, we go our separate ways."

It sounded to Sara as if Val wished they *didn't* go their separate ways.

Kyle dipped a blunt icing knife into another color. "Gramps and Val went to school together. That was a really long time ago," he explained, proving the old adage that little pitchers had big ears.

Out of habit, Val picked up an empty icing dish and took it to the sink to rinse it. "Yep, we sure did."

Sara had the feeling there was a lot Val wasn't saying, that maybe she'd always had a crush on Galen.

"Did you know Nathan's mother?"

The housekeeper's eyes caught hers and held. She must have seen Sara's sincere interest instead of idle curiosity, because she nodded. "Oh, yes. Everyone knew Winifred. She had long black hair and the bluest eyes you've ever seen. I'm not sure how she ended up here, being from England and all. She was trying to find herself before she went back there and settled down. Personally, I think she was tired of the place she grew up, wanted a change, and thought she'd found it here. She was substitute teaching at the high school and working at the feed store part-time when Galen met her."

"I can't imagine a woman leaving three…" Sara stopped and looked down at Kyle. He'd finished icing the last cookie. "Honey, why don't you go wash up? As soon as the icing hardens you can taste one of the cookies."

"Just one?"

"We have to save some for your dad and Gramps."

After a little shrug, Kyle ran to the bathroom.

Val was studying Sara. "You were going to say you couldn't imagine leaving three children behind. I think Winifred felt trapped here in a small town with three kids, and Galen working all the time, though that's no excuse. From what I understand, she had a beau back in England from her earlier days, and I think she decided he could offer her a better life than Galen could. But to never visit, never stay in contact with her kids? I didn't ever understand that, either."

"Maybe she thought they were better off that way."

"Maybe she did think that. But the truth is, I couldn't see Galen letting the boys fly across the ocean to be with her. He was bitter when they broke up." After a moment of silence Val asked, "Aren't you going to be facing the same decision if you turn out to be Kyle's biological mother?"

"Kyle hasn't known me as a mother for the past five years."

"No. But are you going to be able to walk away?"

"No. Not like Nathan's mother did. When I came here, I thought I just needed to see Kyle, but…"

"But you're getting attached."

Sara knew Val would be on Nathan's side, no matter what happened, and she shouldn't be discussing this with her. Turning to the recipe book, she opened to a page near the back. "I thought after lunch Kyle and I could make gingerbread men to put on the tree. When does Nathan usually put it up?"

"Closer to Christmas. The artificial tree's in the basement. He doesn't take any chances with Kyle's asthma."

Val went back to her dusting, and Sara was almost finished washing the baking sheets when Nathan blew in the door with a gust of wind and snow. He seemed to take a moment to get his bearings. The house smelled like vanilla and sugar and Christmas, but he frowned as he came inside.

"Sara wants to know when you're going to put up the Christmas tree," Val commented.

Nathan didn't respond. He seemed frozen for a moment, and then serious lines creased his brow. Unzipping his coat, he asked, "Where's Kyle?"

"He washed up and then went to play in his room," Sara answered. "I think he's counting his arrowheads. He's very proud of the one Ben gave him. I wondered about the Christmas tree," she said, crossing over to him, "because I thought I'd have Kyle help me bake gingerbread cookies to hang on it. We could string popcorn, too—"

"Look, Sara," he interrupted, "don't go all out. It's an artificial tree."

"I know. Val told me. But we can still make it special."

"It's always *been* special. It's *our* Christmas tree."

She didn't know where his anger was coming from, and it *was* anger she heard. "Do you want me to *not* do anything? I don't have to help decorate it if it's something you and Kyle do, a tradition you've started."

Nathan raked his hand through his hair and seemed to be counting to ten, or at least thinking about his reply before he answered. "Sara, you've barged in here with a plan for Christmas. But I don't know if I'm ready to accept it. You're trying to get closer to Kyle, when any friendship you have with him is just going to hurt him when you leave."

"Your brothers are in and out of his life and that doesn't seem to hurt him." She didn't want to get defensive, but something about Nathan's attitude really troubled her right now.

"That's different. If you *are* Kyle's mother, I'm not sure we should tell him."

"You're not serious!"

"I'm very serious. I want you to think about putting

Kyle's interests first, not your own." He strode away from her, stopped and turned. "I'm going to spend some time with him, then go back to the lodge. If you want to make gingerbread cookies for something to do, that's fine. Just remember that next Christmas might be different from this one, no matter what results come back from the DNA test."

Val's eyebrows rose as Nathan exited the room.

Sara was as flummoxed as the housekeeper. Yet there was a difference. She also felt hurt.

Sara was folding one of Kyle's shirts on Friday afternoon when Nathan found her in the laundry room.

"That's Val's job."

"Val's making casseroles for the weekend, so I told her I'd help out. Do you object?"

Conversations between them had been strained since the other day when Nathan had seemed so angry with her plans for Christmas. She knew they were both on edge, waiting for the DNA results, but something else might be bothering him. Even so, she wasn't going to stand by and let him treat her like a stranger, which she wasn't anymore. Not even to him.

He jammed his hands into his jeans pockets and blew out a breath. "No, I don't object. I came to ask you if you'd like to get out for a while. You've been cooped up with Kyle all week. I need some breathing space. I thought we might take the snowmobiles out. Ever ridden one?"

"No. You want me to go with you?"

"Is that so surprising?"

"Considering you've hardly said two words to me for the past few days, yes, it is."

"You're exaggerating. We've had supper together every night."

"Yes, and you talked to Kyle. Or you might have asked me to pass the salt. I'd like to know what you've been thinking about."

"No, you wouldn't like to know."

When she gazed into his eyes, she saw pain there. It drew her to him. Placing Kyle's shirt on the dryer, she stepped closer. "What's the matter?"

After a long pause, he finally told her. "I went to Colleen and Mark's grave on Tuesday. It just hit me, while I was there, that if you *are* Kyle's mother he'll push to spend more time with you, to know more about you. He'll forget the stories I've told him about Colleen. The pictures I have sitting around won't mean a thing."

"You want him to long for a dead mother, rather than having a real one? A living one?"

"This isn't black or white, Sara. This is about a woman I loved. The woman who was going to raise Kyle and Mark. The woman who carried and delivered them and then died because she did."

Sara could see Nathan had made Colleen a saint in his eyes. There was no way she could compete with that. Did she even want to try?

"So you're punishing me for being alive while Colleen isn't?"

"No."

"You've withdrawn, become remote, and don't have a smile for anyone but Kyle. And even that's forced. I think you are punishing me."

Although her words didn't seem to have an effect on him, he asked, "Do you want to go on a snowmobile ride?"

There was restrained patience in his tone and she knew if she wanted to get over this hurdle between them she had to spend some time with him. "I've never ridden a snowmobile, but I'm a fast learner. Just let me put on long underwear and I'll be ready to go."

"You need more than long underwear," he said dryly. "Try a pair of boots, too."

As Nathan left the laundry room, Sara sighed. She supposed a halfhearted joke was better than none.

Sara had ridden a bicycle when she was a teenager, and once or twice she'd been on a horse. But taking a ride on a snowmobile was something she'd never experienced.

After Nathan showed her everything about the controls, she hopped on, eager to get started. She caught him watching her often, and her gaze went to him just as frequently. Even though Nathan might not want anything to do with her, even if he was still in love with his dead wife, he was a man, Sara was a woman, and they were attracted to each other. No amount of explaining away or rationalizing could change that.

The day was gray and overcast, with just a hint of sun glow behind one particularly large cloud. Every once in a while flurries swirled before them. Sara adjusted with one hand the goggles Nathan had lent her, then accelerated a little to keep up with him. She had no idea where they were, and knew she could probably never find her way back, even with a compass. It didn't matter. In spite of her many reservations about getting involved with Nathan, she trusted him. She trusted him to keep her safe and lead her back home.

Home. A Freudian slip. Nathan's house wasn't her home. Rapid Creek wasn't, either.

Yet, did Minneapolis feel like home anymore?

Once she learned the results of the DNA testing, she'd call Joanne. They'd catch up, and Sara would feel back in tune with her life in Minneapolis. At least that's what she told herself.

She and Nathan weren't able to talk, of course, the whole time they rode. But she supposed that was the way he wanted it. Other than his explanations about the snowmobile, he'd avoided any personal discussion, so she was a bit surprised when he slowed his machine and beckoned to her. He was pointing toward a stand of firs and, when she neared them, she slowed and stopped her engine, as he did.

Removing his goggles and helmet, he motioned for her to join him. The snow was about eight inches deep here. Her boots sank in and she laughed as she almost fell with each step.

Nathan approached her and clasped her hand. "We'll have to get you snowshoes."

"You think those would keep me on top?"

"They might. I do have an extra pair of cross-country skis."

"I'm a city girl. I probably couldn't keep them straight in front of me."

"You could if you tried. You were right. You *are* a fast learner. You're handling that snowmobile like a pro."

As they walked side by side, a companionable silence fell over them, until Nathan said, "We don't have far to go."

Suddenly they were at the edge of the trees. Before them lay white fields, birch, firs and a lake, frozen over and glittering in the afternoon light.

"How beautiful."

"This is one of my favorite places, spring, summer, fall or winter. When I'm not using the snowmobile, I have an ATV or I hike out."

Sara felt as if she were gazing into peace and tranquility and a life she didn't know. "Do you bring guests here from the lodge?" She knew Nathan often took parties hiking and fishing.

"No. I never bring anybody here."

They were standing close together, their jackets brushing. "Why did you bring me?"

"I'm not exactly sure, but somehow I knew you'd appreciate it."

Nathan's knit cap covered his ears and came down to his brows. His cheeks were ruddy and the sparkle in his eyes from the scene before them made him seem younger. His face was more relaxed than it had been the past week, the lines around his mouth and eyes not cutting so deep. His black ski jacket against the white background made him look taller and more imposing than he was when they were sitting around the kitchen table with Kyle. In the kitchen, she tried to keep her gaze from his. Now, she didn't. Her focus dropped to the curve of his mouth.

"Sara," he growled.

"What?"

"Stop looking at me like that."

She knew what he meant, because he knew what she wanted. Turning from him, she would have stepped away, but he grasped her shoulder. He drew her closer, until there was no space between them.

"Every time I kiss you, my world shakes," he admitted. "I don't like it."

"Every time you kiss me," she replied, "I feel as if I lose a piece of myself to something I don't understand. It's scary."

"We should stop kissing."

"Yes, we should," she responded softly.

"Chemistry like this doesn't come along often in a man's lifetime."

"Or in a woman's."

"I still wish my wife hadn't died. I can't forget her."

Sara had no response to that. She couldn't say, *It's time you move along. It's time you forget your grief. It's time for you to form a bond with someone new.* Because words didn't matter when feelings were so deep. He'd loved his wife, and Sara admired that about him. So how could she want him to just let go and forget?

"Do you know how beautiful you are? How tempting you are? How much I want to kiss you again?"

If she walked to the snowmobile and drove back to the house, she wouldn't fall in any deeper. If she ignored the chemistry between them, if she patiently waited for the DNA results to be returned, and then made practical, logical decisions, her life would be under control. But with Nathan's eyes boring into hers, the chemistry he spoke of, and most of all her need to be wrapped in his arms, urged her toward him at exactly the same time he reached for her.

The cold should have been a deterrent. The snow flurries should have been a warning. The complete silence, except for the whisper of tree boughs, should have been scary, not inviting. But as Sara's heat mingled with Nathan's, as he lifted her on tiptoe and she wound her arms around his neck, as the down of her jacket pushed into his, she felt she was right where she belonged. His lips were as cold as hers at first, but then quickly heated. The heat became fire, and she sought it and him. Breathing didn't matter as they tasted and explored. Once again, each kiss was different. Each carried risk, and told her she was in over her head.

While they kissed, he unzipped his jacket and then hers. His gloves ended up on the snow as he tunneled inside, warmed his hands on her back and then found the hem of her sweater and slid his palms to her skin. She moaned with the exquisite feel of his fingers on her. They were rough, sensual, scorching.

She wasn't thinking when she pulled off her gloves and let them fall behind him. Unwinding her hands from his neck, she settled them on his waist, then slid them under his sweatshirt. She felt his intake of breath, the tension straining his body. She felt chest hair she'd love to see again, as her fingers played in it.

He broke the kiss, bent his head to nuzzle her neck. She felt as if she might go up in flames. How could that be when cold and snow surrounded them?

Nathan's hands moved higher and cupped her breasts. When he swirled his thumb around her nipple, she wanted her clothes off, no matter what the temperature. As if he read her mind, he unhooked her bra, then held her breasts in his hands.

"Nathan," she breathed, entranced by every new sensation, excited by his fingers on her bare breasts...thrilled by the forbidden pleasure roused by what they were doing. When had she turned into a woman who cared more about satisfaction than sanity or safety?

Since she'd met Nathan.

She had to give him pleasure, too. She didn't want this to be one-sided. Boldly, she unzipped his fly and reached inside. He was aroused, and as soon as her hand was on him, he became even harder.

But then he was pushing away, breathing hard and shaking his head. "No, we can't do this. Not here. And not back home, either. Sara..."

She saw the anguish in his eyes, his need for physical satisfaction with her, but his inability to blot out his memories of the past and what it meant to him. Sara couldn't entice him on when she knew he wanted to go back. If he had his choice, Colleen would be alive. She'd be raising their sons with him. And Sara would have simply been a means to an end.

She didn't want to be a means to anybody's end. She wanted to be Kyle's mother. And she wanted Nathan's heart. However, wanting had never made anybody's dreams come true. Fate had a big part to play in it.

Soon she'd know her fate and Kyle's…and maybe Nathan's, too.

Chapter Eight

At dinner that evening, Sara and Nathan avoided each other's gazes. Fortunately, Kyle chattered on about everything he and Val had done that afternoon, so he didn't notice their silences.

When the phone rang, Nathan was busy helping his son cut his food.

Relieved to get up from the table, Sara went to the counter and answered the phone. "Barclay residence."

"Is that you, Sara?"

"Ted. This is a surprise."

"Not really. You still work here, don't you?"

She hesitated for only a moment. "Yes, of course I do. Is there something you needed on one of my cases?"

"Not exactly. Charles wants to know when you'll be back. He can use you on the team he's setting up to defend the Grayson Company from the age discrimination suit."

"He should have access to this number. I left it for everyone."

She could hear Ted's sigh. "All right, so maybe I just wanted to talk to you myself and find out when you're coming back, exactly. What's your target date?"

"I'm not sure."

"I see. How are you doing?"

"I'm doing fine. How about you? Is any Christmas spirit running around the firm yet?"

"A decorator came in. There's a white tree in the foyer and wreathes on each of the doors. We'll see real Christmas cheer when we get our bonuses. That's another thing. Do you want Charles to send you yours?"

"I'd appreciate that."

"Sara, I really do miss you."

"Ted…"

"I know. I messed up big time with you."

"Nothing's changed," she said softly.

"Maybe *I* have."

She lowered her voice and walked toward the door, away from the table. "You still want children, don't you?"

His silence told her more than words ever could that he hadn't really changed his mind about that. If Ted wanted her, he wanted her temporarily, for pleasure and companionship. She needed something much more permanent than that. She was beginning to believe she wanted Nathan

Barclay in her future. Not just because he was Kyle's father but because she was falling in love with him.

That thought almost struck her dumb.

"Sara."

Licking dry lips, she murmured, "I have to go. I'm in the middle of dinner."

"I'm sorry I interrupted, but I *am* looking forward to you coming back. This place isn't the same without you."

She didn't believe that for a minute. She knew very well that if she dropped off the face of the earth she could be replaced in twenty-four hours. Maybe not even that long.

When Sara returned to the kitchen table, Kyle had finished with his dinner, but his fingers were sticky.

"Wash your hands," Nathan told him, "then we'll see if we can find some dessert."

"I want a Christmas star."

"If there are any left. Val said you were eating all of those first."

With a grin that would melt any parent's heart, Kyle ran off to the bathroom.

Sara resumed her place at the table, but pushed her plate away. She'd lost her appetite.

"A phone call from home?" Nathan asked, watching her carefully.

"Not exactly. Someone at work."

"Someone you care about?"

"I thought I did. We dated for a while." She didn't want to get into this with Nathan. She *was* falling in love with him. But whether she was Kyle's mother or not, Nathan liked being a father. She imagined he'd want more children with any woman he became involved with. He couldn't have them with her.

Her eyes filmed over with tears. As she closed them, she pushed away from the table. Turning to the cupboard, she took out a filter. "Would you like coffee?" she somehow managed to ask.

"Sure. Coffee and cookies should be a great way to end the day. Better make it decaf, though, if we want to get any sleep tonight."

She doubted if she was going to sleep. Too many thoughts were roaming around in her head. Too many questions with no answers. Too many problems with no solutions.

"I'm thinking about going north tomorrow to see Sam. It's about a four-hour drive. Would you like to come along?"

She swung around, surprised. "You want me to go with you?"

"I could use the company. Besides that, I'd like you to help me convince him to come home for Christmas. You're good with people. Maybe you'd be good with him. When he gets an idea in his head, nothing can budge him, usually. But if the two of us tackle him, maybe we can convince him. We can stay overnight and come home the next day. The only problem is, the cabin is pretty rustic. Do you like to go camping?"

"I've never been camping."

"Uh-oh. There's a wood stove insert in the fireplace for heat, running water and electricity. But not much else."

She shouldn't even consider going. But she wanted to

spend time with Nathan. They'd be away from Kyle and she could see if what she felt was all tied up with his little boy, or with Nathan himself.

"If I take him provisions, we'll be sure to have food, too. Even if he doesn't come back with us, I'll make certain he's okay. Are you game?"

Without any hesitation now, she agreed. "I'm game."

She'd taken a risk coming to Rapid Creek in the first place. Going north with Nathan would put her heart in further jeopardy. But she had to find out what was real and what wasn't. She had to find out if the love she felt for Nathan could grow—and could be returned.

In spite of herself, she couldn't stop hoping.

"You've got everything here but the kitchen sink," Val decided, as she and Sara sorted and packed the groceries that Nathan had bought, stowing perishables in the cooler.

"I think Nathan wants to make sure Sam has enough provisions if he doesn't come back for Christmas."

"That woman hurt him badly. I hope she *never* comes back to Rapid Creek."

"She left after they broke up?"

"She sure did. But that didn't help Sam much."

Kyle proudly handed Sara cans of dog food. "Don't forget Patches's food. He eats a lot."

Sara laughed. "Your dad already has a bag of kibbles for him in the SUV."

When the buzzer sounded on the stove, Val picked up her oven mitts and took out a cherry pie.

"Is that for Kyle or Galen?" Sara asked. Galen was going to stay overnight with his grandson.

"Both of them. They wanted hamburgers and French fries for supper, so that's what they're getting."

"Are you going to eat with them?"

"Land sakes, no. I'll just make supper and leave."

"Why don't you stay and keep them company? I'm sure Kyle would like that. Probably Galen, too."

Suddenly Val looked flustered. "Oh, I can't do that. Galen would think I'm pushing myself on him."

"Because you join them for supper? That's not pushing. Did you ever think that Galen might be lonely and would enjoy your company?"

"Well, no, I never did. I figured if he wanted my company he'd ask for it."

"Maybe he's afraid you don't want to spend time with him."

The door opened and Nathan came in. His gaze met Sara's, and she wondered again if she'd made the right decision, going with him. Sometimes when he looked at her, her heart almost stopped.

"Are you ready?" he asked.

"Almost. Did you get the bedrolls?" She didn't know what sleeping conditions were going to be like at the cabin, but Nathan had told her they'd be prepared.

"Bedrolls are already packed in the back."

Sara went to the peg by the door and plucked off her coat. Kyle watched her as she slid into it, zipped it, took her hat from the pocket and pulled it onto her head.

He ran over to her and hugged her hard. "I'm gonna miss you."

The lump in Sara's throat was hard to talk around. "I'm going to miss you, too. But we won't be gone that long."

"You're coming back tomorrow. Right?"

Nathan crossed to his son and laid his hand on his shoulder. "It might be tomorrow evening. It takes a long time to drive back here from the cabin, and we don't know what kind of weather we'll run into. But we *will* be back tomorrow."

When Nathan stooped down, Kyle gave him a huge hug, too. "Gramps and I are going to have fun tonight. He said he'll teach me how to whistle."

"That might take awhile to learn," Nathan said seriously.

As he stood, Val laid one hand on top of Kyle's head. "Don't you worry. We'll make the time pass."

"His new inhaler is on the sink in the bathroom," Nathan reminded her.

"I know. His old one's right here." She pointed to the counter near the canisters. "And I've got the doctor's number and can always call 911. But we aren't going to need to do that. We'll be fine, Nathan, really. You know your dad will be as protective of Kyle as he was of you and your brothers."

"I know."

Sara imagined how hard it was for Nathan to leave his son in someone else's care. He must really be concerned about his brother to go north now, so near to Christmas.

As if reading her thoughts, he told Kyle, "As soon as

we get back I'll bring up the tree from the basement."
After another hug and a wave, Nathan picked up the cooler
and let Sara precede him outside.

On the drive north, Nathan kept seeing the picture in
his head of Kyle hugging Sara, hearing Kyle say, "I'll
miss you." His son was getting attached to her. Whether
it was good or bad, it was a fact. She handled Kyle so
deftly, so easily, as if she'd been with children all her life.
She'd make a wonderful mother.

Sara broke into his reverie about an hour into the trip.
"I think Val likes your dad…a lot."

Nathan shot her a glance. "What makes you think that?"

She gave him one of those men-are-so-blind looks. "A
few comments she's made. I think she's had feelings for
him since before he married your mother."

Nathan thought about it. Although he didn't want to get
into a discussion about his mom, his father was a different story. "They did go to school together."

"That's what Val said. Has your dad ever considered
getting married again?"

"Never. He hasn't even dated. I talked to him about it
once, after Sam went to college. We were all gone from
home. I figured he might be lonely. But he simply told me
he had no desire to be in the company of a woman. One
would cause too much disturbance in his life. He liked
doing things the way he wanted to do them, and didn't want
to change. Since he opened the lodge, he's been busy with
that. I hope you're not thinking about playing matchmaker."

"Of course not," she answered softly.

"Good. Because throwing people together doesn't make them closer. Val and Dad are friends. I wouldn't want to see anything happen to that."

"Maybe your dad has never considered dating Val because he *is* so close to her. Maybe if he just opened his eyes, he could have a partner for the rest of his life."

"Don't you have enough concerns of your own to think about without adding Dad's?"

Suddenly, Nathan braked and pointed to his left. "Look." Along the side of the road were two elk, blending in with their surroundings. They stood perfectly still for a moment, eyeing the car, then they lumbered off into the forest.

"Were they moose?" Sara asked.

Nathan laughed. "Any self-respecting moose would consider that an insult. No, they're elk. You really are a city girl, aren't you?"

She frowned. "Maybe. But now I'll know an elk from a moose if I see another one." Nathan couldn't help laughing again. And it felt good to do so. Sure, Kyle made him smile. But that genuine, free laughter had been caged inside of him for a long time. It was great to let it out.

Sara was smiling at him. "I'm glad I'm so funny."

"You're not funny, Sara, you're real. And I like that." He liked it too damn much.

The scenery was pure Minnesota winter—fir trees coated with snow, icy lakes, white fields as far as the eye could see, gray sky that portended more snow, which began falling an hour from their destination.

Sara lifted her purse from the floor. "Do you mind if I play a CD? I brought a Christmas one."

The wipers were working to keep the frenzied flurries from the windshield. The heater blew warmth through the SUV. Nathan could feel Sara's expectant gaze on him. He was aware of her slender body, angled toward him. He noticed the silkiness of her hair as she turned her head and strands swung along her cheek. Christmas music always stabbed him where he hurt. But he couldn't be a Scrooge, could he?

"Take it out of its case and I'll slip it in," he said gruffly. He was closer to the unit than she was.

When she handed the CD to him, their fingers touched. The electricity almost made him drop the disk. But he held on to it, slid it into the player and pressed the button to start it. Soon, instrumental strains were floating through the car.

"Do you really *like* Christmas, or are you just enjoying it because of Kyle?" he asked her, genuinely curious.

"I love the holidays. Mom and I had traditions. We never had a lot of money, so some were born out of necessity. We'd always put our tree up on Christmas Eve because that's when they went on sale and we could get one for very little cost. We made the ornaments together the week before. It's amazing what we could do with glue, glitter and construction paper. We belonged to one of those grocery store clubs, so anything we bought gave us points toward the holiday turkey."

"And your mom taught you how to cook it," Nathan guessed with a smile.

"Yes, she did. She'd invite anyone who didn't have a place to go on Christmas. When I was little, it might be a friend from her work. Neighbors joined us. When I was in college, I had a friend whose parents traveled over the holidays. She came home with me a couple of times. I remember one year we learned there was a family down the street who was having a rough time of it. The husband had been laid off work and they had three kids under five, so the wife couldn't get a job. Mom invited them to have Christmas dinner with us. It sure wasn't a fix for their situation, but that day helped. Christmas was about the church service and sharing what we had with others. Gifts didn't enter into it very much," she added, her voice husky with reminiscence.

"Speaking of churches and Christmas, if you're still here, would you like to help decorate the church the weekend before Christmas? We're always looking for volunteers."

"Sure. I'd like to help." After a pause, she asked, "What do you remember most about your Christmases as a kid?"

Nathan could easily see where Sara got her giving spirit. Her mother had taught her well. "I think I've blocked out the earlier years. Our mother always insisted she had to go shopping in Minneapolis, and she'd take that yearly trip, stay for a week, then come home with a carload of packages. But then she and Dad would argue about the money she'd spent. He couldn't understand why she couldn't find what she needed in Rapid Creek. She seemed to count the days every year until she'd have that week away, and I always got the impression that coming back to us was a huge letdown. Dad could sense that. It made him uneasy and sad that he couldn't give her what she needed."

"A life bigger than Rapid Creek?" Sara asked.

"Yeah. That was all *he* knew. That was all he *wanted* to know."

"I guess when she married your dad she thought she could be happy in Rapid Creek."

"She married Dad because she was pregnant with me. If she hadn't gotten pregnant, they probably wouldn't have married."

Perceptively, Sara asked, "Did you feel responsible when she left?"

"When I was a kid, maybe first grade, I heard them arguing. My mother told Dad he'd given their baby a name, but she'd never wanted me. She'd only had Ben and Sam because she'd been trying to delude herself into thinking a husband and family could satisfy her. But a husband and kids were no substitute for a doctorate."

"Oh, Nathan, I'm sorry. A child should never hear anything like that."

"Actually, I think it prepared me for when she left. I never had any doubt that Dad was solid, that he loved me and Sam and Ben. Our home was in Rapid Creek, and that would never change. It was comforting, for a kid whose mother wanted to be anyplace but where she was."

"Did you ever talk to Ben and Sam about her?"

"Not before she left. They were younger than me. I didn't want them to know she didn't want any of us. We just rallied around Dad and knew our life was with him.

Christmases after she left were about presents and toys, to make up for not having a mother."

"What about as you got older?"

"Christmases became quieter. Dad was a decent cook, but we helped him more. Soon we were the ones who decorated and put up the tree. I think he really lost his Christmas spirit until Colleen and I married. We'd come back here for the holidays, so would Ben and Sam, and Dad really seemed to enjoy it. After Colleen died, we had to make Christmas good for Kyle. Children definitely are the spirit of Christmas."

The windshield wipers swished snow away. After a few moments of staring ahead, Sara asked, "Did Colleen have anything special she liked to do? Something you've tried to keep alive for Kyle?"

Either Sara was the bravest person he knew, or the most foolhardy. Even his brothers didn't bring up this subject. Trying to stay emotionally detached, he explained, "Each year she bought a particularly special ornament for the tree. I do that now with Kyle. We go into town to the Christmas shop and find an ornament he really likes."

"Does he know it was his mother's tradition?"

"Yes, he does."

"Did she like to cook? To bake?"

"No, Colleen wasn't into any of that, though I would expect as our kids got older she might have learned to like it. Icing cookies with kids is something special."

He could see from Sara's face that she thought it was, too. He remembered the day he'd come into the kitchen after she and Kyle had iced cookies…when she'd wanted to make the gingerbread men. They were ready and waiting in the tin now. He just needed to put up the tree. Maybe he'd been postponing the inevitable.

"It's hard for you to see me with Kyle this Christmas, isn't it?" Sara murmured.

"I want Kyle to experience everything he can about Christmas. You're part of that this year."

"You didn't answer my question."

"Sure, it's hard. Every holiday I imagine Colleen with him. I imagine what Kyle would have been like if he had a twin brother. *Hard* isn't the word to cover it."

Sara kept silent after that burst of truth. She'd wanted to know, and he'd told her.

However, as the snow crunched under his tires, as it deepened the farther they went, as the minutes ticked by more slowly, he realized that memories weren't enough. They were almost too alive sometimes, and revisiting them only hurt. Did he do it so he could stay connected to the pain? And to Colleen? If he let go of the grief, would he lose her, too?

He'd thought he'd moved on. He'd thought he'd made a life for him and Kyle. But the results of the DNA test could change everything. If Sara was Kyle's mother, they'd have to include her. It would only be fair to Kyle.

On the other hand, how much would she want to be included? Her life in Minneapolis, her connection to that guy she worked with—he'd heard a different note in her voice when she'd spoken to Ted—might just make her a rare visitor to Rapid Creek.

Wasn't that what Nathan wanted? Hadn't he hoped she wasn't Kyle's mother, and his life could go back to the way it was before she'd walked into the lodge?

Glancing at her now, her perfect profile, the softness of her skin, the tilt of her head and the curve of her shoulder, he found one thought predominating. He wanted to take her to bed. Whether it was right or wrong, had to do with the past or the present, he didn't care.

Maybe if he gave in to his desire to sleep with Sara he'd satisfy his curiosity and craving for her, and both would go away.

Then he could live in peace again.

Peace? Even if it cost Kyle a mother?

Peace on his own terms; that was the Christmas gift Nathan wanted.

The SUV zigzagged to a stop beside a rustic log cabin. Through the shower of snowflakes, Sara eyed the place, which couldn't be more than two rooms. Smoke wisped upward from the chimney.

She concentrated on her surroundings as Nathan pulled up beside Sam's van so she wouldn't think about everything Nathan had said. He was still steeped in the past; his memories chained him to it. She could get so hurt if she became involved with him. Yet her heart had led her most of her life, and she couldn't seem to stop it now.

"He might not be happy we're here," Nathan warned her, breaking into her thoughts.

"On the other hand, he might be ready to have some company."

"Are you one of those eternal optimists?"

"Whenever I can be."

As soon as they opened their doors, they heard barking from inside the cabin.

"That's Patches," Nathan explained.

"Does he have ESP?"

"Sometimes I think he does. He didn't like Alicia. Growled every time she came close. Sam actually had to put him out of the bedroom when they…well, you know."

"I didn't know I was going to have to pass a Patches test. This could be interesting. I've never been around many animals. But I guess they're like kids."

Nathan gazed at her over the top of the SUV. "Sam treats all of the animals at the clinic like kids. Maybe you two are on the same wavelength." Wading to the rear of the car through the snow, he opened the back. "I'm going to get the cooler. If he sees I brought provisions, maybe he won't send us packing."

"I can help."

"No, that's okay. Watch yourself on the front step. It gets icy."

Sara hadn't even reached the step when the door opened. Patches appeared beside his master, barking to let the whole world know they had company.

Sam scowled as he asked Nathan, "What are *you* doing here?"

Chapter Nine

"I brought supplies," Nathan explained with a huge smile. "Aren't you about running out? Doesn't Patches need kibbles?"

Sam narrowed his eyes. "I bought a twenty-five pound bag for him before I drove up. I have enough canned goods for myself to last until June. But if you brought something Val made…"

Sara stepped onto the porch as Patches came forward to sniff at her coat and her boots. "I brought gingerbread men and sugar cookies Kyle decorated. There might even be half a chocolate cake from Val."

Nathan watched his brother's attention slide to Sara. What man's wouldn't?

Without the hint of a smile, Sam held out his hand to shake hers. "Anyone bringing me half a chocolate cake is more than welcome."

"I'm Sara Hobart."

Sam's gaze shifted to Nathan again, as he looked for an explanation.

Knowing his brother wanted quick, pertinent information, he explained bluntly. "Sara could be Kyle's mother. She donated her eggs, and the dates are right. We're having a DNA test done to make sure."

After sliding off her glove, Sara held her hand out to Patches. He sniffed it, put his head under it and rubbed against her.

"He wants his ears scratched, and will do anything to make that happen. Come on in out of the snow. The cabin is a mess," Sam warned them.

He wasn't underestimating the state of the cabin, but Sam looked as if he belonged here. His hair was long and shaggy, and he'd let his beard grow. With his Green Bay Packers sweatshirt and jeans with the holes in the knees, he appeared as uncivilized as his surroundings. Yet that didn't seem to put Sara off, Nathan noticed with a smile.

"It looks as if you're working," she commented.

There were magazines and books stacked everywhere, notebooks and sheets of paper with scratchings and notes. Sam's laptop sat on a bare wooden table near one wall, his printer plugged into one of the few receptacles.

Their father had furnished the cabin years ago with a green-and-red-plaid, secondhand sofa, and a navy-blue armchair whose covering looked gray and dusty after all these years. The kitchen area contained a microwave and a two-burner range. A small sink was positioned under a window that looked out on the side yard. Only three feet high, the refrigerator had boxes stacked on top of it that held some of Sam's supplies, including gallon jugs of water. There were a few knotty pine cupboards. The plank floor was pine, too. A braided, multicolored area rug curved under the sofa, and Patches's big bed, in red-and-black plaid, sat to the side of it. Sam might not care if *he* had creature comforts, but he'd provide them for his dog.

Nathan set the cooler on top of some papers on the counter.

"Wait a minute! Don't cover up my notes! I'll never find them again."

"Notes on what?" Nathan asked dryly.

"On building a veterinary clinic in Haiti." Sam addressed Sara. "So are you staying at the lodge?"

"No. I'm staying with Nathan and Kyle."

Sam's surprise was obvious.

"When Sara first approached me about all of this, when she first met Kyle, they connected," Nathan admitted. "Since there's a distinct possibility she could be his mother, we decided this arrangement would work best."

Sam shifted the cooler aside and gathered up his papers. "That's got to be different for you, having someone besides Val around."

"I'm staying until we get the results of the DNA test," Sara added, "I have a job in Minneapolis to get back to."

Over his shoulder, Sam asked, "What do you do?"

"I'm a lawyer with a corporate firm."

Taking his papers to the table, Sam added them to a stack there. "I guess you two didn't come for a five-minute visit."

"Not hardly," Nathan muttered. "Tell me you don't need a little company, at least for one night."

"I don't think you came up here to keep me company for a night."

"I have more supplies in the car. I'll bring them in." Ignoring Sam's tone, Nathan started toward the door.

"I know why you came," his brother called after him. "You think you're going to talk me into going back with you. Or coming home for Christmas. It's not going to happen."

Nathan stopped at the threshold. "Why would you want to stay up here for the holiday when you could be with your family?"

"Right now, I just need to be away from people, from their concern, from their questions. And from all the warm and cuddly feelings surrounding the holidays. I am *not* in a celebrating mood, and I'm definitely not full of good cheer."

"Dad's worried about you."

"Dad, you, Ben. But *stop worrying*. Look at me. I'm eating. I'm sleeping. I'm exercising. I'm researching. I'm not wasting away. I'm not contemplating my toes. I'll be back when I'm ready to come back. Are we clear?"

Nathan knew that tone. He also knew Sam's stubborn streak was even worse than Ben's. There was no point arguing with him now, especially in front of Sara. Maybe later he could reason with him.

Patches had sidled up to Sara and collapsed in front of her. Absently, she caressed the dog's head as she listened to the brothers' conversation.

Sam grinned at his dog. "Hey, pooch. Have you defected to the fairer sex?"

Patches cocked his head.

"All right. I'll defer to your judgment."

"The food in that cooler has to go in the refrigerator," Nathan announced as he opened the door and went outside.

"I'll be right out, as soon as I get my boots on," Sam called.

While Nathan's brother took off his sneakers and sat on the sofa to put on his boots, Sara opened the cooler. "Nathan said that, like Kyle, you're fond of hot dogs, so that's what we brought. But I made a pot of homemade baked beans to go with them. The batch is big, so you'll have enough to last you a few days. I brought some fresh vegetables, too, since there isn't a store nearby—carrots, celery, cucumbers. There's a soup bone for Patches. That was Val's idea. I could start unpacking everything—"

"Easy, Sara. I'm not going to grill you. Not if *you* don't grill *me*."

She looked into Sam's steady brown eyes. He shot from the hip, just like Nathan, and she might as well do the same. "Everyone handles disappointment or loss in their own way. If this is where you need to be and what you need to do, no one should try to convince you otherwise."

"You know what happened?"

"Yes. But only because your family *is* worried about you, not because they were talking behind your back, or confided anything to me."

"So why did you come up here with Nathan?"

"He wanted company."

"Nathan wouldn't lock himself in a car with a woman unless he had a very good reason."

Sara felt her cheeks heating up, and it wasn't from the warmth coming from the wood stove insert.

"Hmm," Sam said. "That's a subject we can explore after I get to know you better." His boots on his feet now, he grabbed his coat from the back of the armchair and headed outside to help his brother.

Patches traipsed after his master.

Turning to the cooler, Sara began unpacking.

A few minutes later, the brothers reappeared with the rest of the supplies. Although the microwave would have been the obvious way to cook the hot dogs, Nathan insisted he'd be chef for the night. He split them, pan-fried them while the beans warmed, then popped a slice of cheese in each until it melted. The result, Sara decided, was delicious. They folded them in rolls, added mustard or ketchup, and enjoyed them with the baked beans and carrot sticks.

"Great supper!" Sam declared after he'd finished his third hot dog. "Better than the beef stew I was going to warm up out of a can."

"So you're not sorry we came?" Nathan asked mischievously.

"No, not sorry. I just wish you could convince Dad and Ben that I'm fine."

"How much longer are you going to stay up here? Really. Eric's got to have his hands full, covering for you. I saw Corrie at the gas station. She asked about you."

"She's wasting her talent, being a vet tech. She should go back to school and finish her degree."

"Do you know why she dropped out?"

"Nope. We never talked about that."

"She's worked for you for what? Three years?"

"About that. We joke around, talk about the animals, but never delve into personal history."

Since there was only one chair at the table, the three of them were sitting on the sofa. Now Sam reached for his slice of chocolate cake on the coffee table. "Tell Eric I'll be back in a month or so."

"You should tell him yourself."

"Cell phones don't work here unless I drive ten miles up the road. When I come back to Rapid Creek, I'll make sure Eric takes a nice long vacation. So…" he drawled. "What are we going to do after supper? Play charades?"

"We can do better than that." Nathan reached into the pocket of his jacket, which he'd hung on the corner of the sofa. He pulled out a deck of cards. "Either gin or poker."

They decided on poker.

Two hours later, Sam sank back against the sofa cushion. "Sara won all my twigs. Who would believe that someone so angelic looking could bluff so well?"

She smiled, knowing most of his exasperation was put

on. "I think maybe you let me win. Either that or the two of you have something else on your mind."

As soon as she said it, she knew she shouldn't have. Although it was true that both Sam and Nathan had seemed distracted while they were playing poker, she should have let sleeping dogs lie. She had no idea what either of them was thinking, and from the looks on their faces now, they weren't going to tell her.

Sam levered himself up off the sofa. "I have to let Patches out. But before I do, we have to decide on sleeping arrangements. You two can have the twin beds in the bedroom if you'd like. It'll be colder than in here, but you'll probably be more comfortable. I can bunk on the couch."

"We brought bedrolls," Sara said. "We don't want to put you out of your bedroom."

"No big deal. Sometimes when I work late I crash out here, anyway."

"That sounds like a plan," Nathan agreed, getting to his feet. "Sara, I'll go out with Sam if you want to get ready for bed and slip under the covers. Is fifteen minutes okay?"

Although she was living under the same roof with Nathan for the time being, he didn't know her nightly ritual. It wasn't much of one. She brushed her teeth, washed her face, smoothed on some lotion, then headed for bed. "Fifteen minutes is fine."

Rising from the sofa, she picked up her bag and headed for the small bathroom. At the door she turned to Sam. "If you need some of those twigs, I'll lend them to you so you have a stake for your next poker game."

He laughed, gave her a wink, then called to Patches, who was asleep in his bed.

The whole time Sara was washing her face, brushing her teeth and applying lotion, she told herself she shouldn't be nervous about sleeping in the same room with Nathan. There was nothing to be concerned about. She'd be in bed already. He'd climb into his. They'd turn off the light and they'd go to sleep. Simple. Right?

She should have known nothing with Nathan would be simple.

Since one of the beds had a cotton spread thrown over it, but no sheets or blankets, Sara untied the bedroll and spread it out on the mattress. Donning her flannel nightgown, leaving her fuzzy pink stocking slippers on her feet for extra warmth, she pulled the sleeping bag over her and tried to snuggle in. The pillowcase was cold under her cheek, but she knew she'd warm up soon. Still, she shivered and curled up.

When Nathan entered the bedroom, she opened her eyes…and knew she shouldn't have. He was wearing black flannel shorts, but his torso was bare. Her eyes didn't know whether to settle on all that thick chest hair or slide down his hair-roughened legs.

"Comfortable?" he asked as he sat on the metal-frame bed, then reached to turn off the small lamp on the nightstand.

"I'm fine," she answered, her voice a bit unsteady.

When they were in darkness, staring at the moon shining in the window, silence stretched between them.

Finally she heard Nathan's bed squeak, and guessed he was turning on his side. To her surprise, he asked, "Do you date much?"

Her response was spontaneous and truthful. "No."

"Why not?"

That answer was uncomplicated. "In college I focused on earning my degree, getting into a good law school. Law school was tough. I held a part-time job, and what with that and keeping up with my study group, I couldn't fit in a social life. After I joined the law firm…well, working eighty hours a week doesn't leave much time for dates."

"But you dated…Ted?"

"Yes. For a while. That was before the accident. Afterward, I reexamined everything in my life."

If she told him that Ted had walked away, would she find out how Nathan felt about having more children? Did she really want to have that conversation now, though? Here? When she couldn't look into his eyes or see his face? When she felt awkward and uncomfortable because his brother was right outside, in the living room?

Changing the subject, she asked in a low tone, "Are you still worried about Sam? He really does seem to be okay. He just wants some time alone."

"He puts up a good front, but he's not okay. He's not the recluse type. Walking away from his practice with Eric like that—it's not like him."

"Maybe he's evaluating his life, trying to figure out if what he's been doing is what he wants to go on doing."

"You two seem to get along."

"I like him. He's much more approachable than Ben."

"You've got that right. Ben's the family cynic. You have to prove yourself to Ben before he'll let you in. Sam, on the other hand, decides when he meets you if he likes you or not. If he does, you're in."

"What about you? Are you like Ben or Sam?"

"I've never thought about it. I guess I'm a combination of the two. More cautious than Sam, but not as guarded as Ben."

"Thank you for letting me in, Nathan. I mean, you could have made everything so much harder. You could have kept me from Kyle. I don't know what's going to happen, but I'll always be grateful you gave me this opportunity to get to know him."

This time Nathan's silence lasted until they both fell asleep.

Sara wasn't sure what awakened her, whether it was a noise, the rustle of covers, Nathan getting up and going out of the room, or the cold. She was shivering so badly her teeth were chattering. She heard water running in the bathroom, and then Nathan coming back, his tall figure lean and fit and muscled in the shadowy room.

"What time is it?" she asked, trying to keep her voice steady.

"About two."

At least four or five more hours of this. How could she go to sleep when she was freezing? "Is it warmer in the other room?"

"Not much. The fire died down. Sam conserves wood at night. Are you cold?"

"Aren't you?"

He came over to her bed and hunched down beside her. "No, I'm not. But I've spent lots of nights here over the years. There *is* a solution."

"What?"

"Come over and sleep with me. We'll combine our body heat."

She could tell from his tone that he was serious.

"What are you afraid of, Sara? I promise I'll be the perfect gentleman. I'll put on my jeans. Would that make you feel safer?"

Another shiver ran up her spine. "All right. We can try it. But with two people in a twin bed, you might not get any sleep."

"I'll sleep."

He didn't wait for her to change her mind, but grabbed his jeans from a chair near the window and pulled them on.

There were two reasons to crawl into that bed with him. One was getting warm, the other was just being close to him. If Nathan warmed her body, could she warm his heart?

She felt awkward as he stretched out first, sliding against the wall. But the floor was cold under her feet. She had goose bumps all over and she wasn't going to stand there and freeze. She sat down on the edge of the bed, then carefully lay on her side, taking up as little room as she could.

"You'll fall off," he teased, his breath warm against her ear.

"I want you to have enough room."

"It's combined body heat that will make you warm." His arm went around her waist as he pulled her a little closer. His hand brushed hers. "You *are* cold. Come on, try to relax."

Relax? When his long, hard body was stretched out within kissing distance? When her heart was beating so fast she could hardly catch her breath?

He stroked the back of her head. "It's okay, Sara. All we're going to do is sleep."

All they were going to do was sleep.

Maybe that was the problem. Maybe she wanted to do more than sleep. Yet if she made love with Nathan, she'd have to face all kinds of unanswered questions.

As his hand slid over her hair time and time again, stroking gently, she felt her body uncoil. The stiffness left her limbs and she nestled against him, needing his heat.

"That's it," he murmured. "You're safe with me, Sara. I promise."

In her heart she knew Nathan was a man of his word. Sleep soon overtook her, and she gave herself up to it.

When Sara awakened, her position from the night before had changed. In their sleep, and possibly in their desire to be warm, she and Nathan had cuddled together. He was on his back, his arm around her and her head on his chest. Her arm was around him. He was so thoroughly male, with his thick mat of chest hair, muscled arms, masculine scent. If she tilted her head she could kiss his shoulder. If she did—

"Ready to get up?" he asked.

"How did you know I was awake?"

"Your breathing changed."

He noticed everything. And if he noticed how much she enjoyed lying there with him, her arm tight around him, she could be in big trouble.

He was perfectly still, and as she rearranged herself so she could sit up, she found out why. Without the cover she could see the evidence of his arousal.

Their gazes met…and held. Still, he didn't move. "Go ahead and use the bathroom to get dressed. Let me know when you're finished."

She wanted to thank him for keeping her warm last night. But his expression was strained, his body taut, and she decided now wasn't a good time. Hurriedly picking up her bag, then grabbing yesterday's clothes, which were hanging on a hook on the door, she practically ran to the bathroom.

Sara felt as if she and Nathan were standing on the top of a volcano. It was just waiting to erupt. The wrong look, word or touch could set it into motion, and then they'd have to deal with the aftermath.

Her hands shook as she picked up her toothbrush, and the trembling wasn't from the cold.

Before Sara finished brushing her teeth, there was a knock on the bathroom door. It was Nathan. "Sam wants to say goodbye. He's taking Patches out for a walk and we'll probably be gone when he gets back."

Her flannel nightgown was heavy enough and long enough that nothing showed. When she opened the door to the bathroom, she could feel a rush of heat and realized the stove was stoked high again.

Sam was already dressed in blue ski gear, his snow-shoes balanced on his shoulder. "Thanks for coming along with Nathan. Poker's a lot more fun with three than with two."

"It was good to meet you."

"Same here. The snow stopped soon after you arrived, so you should be okay going home. Keep her safe," he said to Nathan.

Patches trotted over to Sara, licked her hand as if to say goodbye, too, then followed his master out the door.

Although Sara's body was covered with flannel, although she'd spent the night in Nathan's arms, she felt self-conscious as he looked at her. Maybe that was because there was heat in his eyes. Or because his waistband wasn't buttoned and his chest was bare. Or because they were alone in the cabin, Sam was trekking away, and there was no one else around for miles.

"I do like your brother," she said, trying to make conversation and get over the sudden awkwardness at being alone in the cabin.

"I think the feeling is mutual." Nathan crossed to her. "He would have been a bear if I had come up here by myself. Probably would have thrown me out."

"I doubt that…*if* you'd brought the chocolate cake."

The pulsing silence in the cabin seemed to draw them closer together and wrap them in intimacy. "Sam gulped down a couple of doughnuts when he was getting dressed, but there's a half dozen left for us. I can put coffee on."

"A sugar and caffeine high." Her voice was decidedly shaky.

"Sara…" Nathan groaned.

She heard the same longing in his voice that she'd felt as she'd cuddled with him last night…the longing that tugged at her whenever they were in the same room.

He tipped her chin up, stared into her eyes and then kissed her. It was a kiss that had waited through a long drive in the snow. That had been anticipated between poker hands. That might have happened when she'd crawled into bed with him, but they'd both been dead set against letting it.

Willpower only went so far.

The circumstances and opportunity to let that kiss happen right now were undeniable. They'd never really been alone before, not like this. But now…Nathan was a man and she was a woman, and the chemistry between them was too irresistible to ignore.

The kiss started hot and flamed hotter. Nathan's hands danced up and down her back as hers explored his. She didn't know who made the first intimate move, but suddenly his palms were on her breasts and hers were sliding under his waistband. Pure physical need seemed to drive them both as their lips clung, their tongues danced, their bodies sought closer contact. Taking handfuls of her nightgown into closed fists, Nathan lifted it inch by inch until her backside was bare. Then he pushed her tight against his arousal. She'd never felt anything so erotic. She'd never wanted a union with a man more. They didn't think twice about where they were, or comfort, or finding a soft spot to land. Once he'd raised her nightgown over her head and dropped it, once she'd pushed down his jeans and shorts and he'd kicked them aside, they were liquid together, melting into each other.

Nathan pushed the coffee table away, and they dropped onto the rug by the sofa. They didn't speak, just gave pleasure and took it. Nathan's tongue laved her breasts while she caressed him with her palm. His groan was gut deep. Her moan pulled the longing out of her soul into the light where she could feel it, see it, touch it and know it was connected to love. Nathan gently touched and kissed the scars from her surgery, then rose above her. She spread her legs.

He thrust inside of her and she wrapped her arms around him, holding on tight.

A few moments later, when Nathan withdrew, she felt tears come to her eyes. He wasn't going to stop, was he? He hadn't changed his mind, had he? But then he was thrusting into her again, harder and deeper. Even if he had doubts, she knew he couldn't stop, any more than she could. Her climax began in tingling waves that radiated through her body. One hit and she drowned in the pleasure of it. But then another overlapped the first, and a third one made every muscle in her body tremble. The burst of sensation was so overwhelming she squeezed her eyes shut, dug her nails into Nathan's back and rode with the thrill until it faded into trembling and exhaustion. Nathan thrust into her once more and she contracted around him. He shuddered…shuddered again…and went still.

As soon as Sara's world stopped spinning, she opened her eyes.

Nathan lifted his head from where it had dropped on her shoulder, and she could see concern in his expression. "Are you okay?"

"I'm fine. How about you?"

His lips weren't far from hers, but he didn't kiss her. He lifted himself away and sat on the floor beside her. There was a shift in the room. The intimacy they'd shared vanished.

After a few moments he let out a long breath. "We should pack up and get going."

"We need to talk about this…about what just happened."

As he met her gaze, she glimpsed the turmoil inside him. With foreboding, she suspected what was coming, but when he said the words, she wasn't ready for them.

"For now, I think it's better if we don't. We know what it was, Sara. We've been building up to it since we met. It was a release of the pressure we both felt. But that doesn't mean it should happen again."

The stoic expression on his face told her he was resisting any tender feelings. He was pushing away any emotions that might resemble what he'd once felt for his wife.

Sara had made mistakes in her life, but right now, this one felt like the biggest of all.

Chapter Ten

On Thursday evening, Sara had left the door to the bathroom ajar, just in case Kyle called for her. He hadn't seemed upset that his father wasn't home. Nathan had called to ask if she would mind putting Kyle to bed. Of course she didn't mind! Although Nathan had reminded her where Kyle's inhalers were located, he hadn't mentioned why he wouldn't be home. She didn't have the right to ask. As nine o'clock approached, she'd followed Kyle's usual bedtime routine.

Now she was trying to relax the tension from her body by taking a bubble bath. She'd been tense ever since…

Ever since Nathan had decided what happened between them last Sunday at Sam's cabin had been a mistake.

She'd never attribute ulterior motives to Nathan. He was a stand-up kind of guy. If he'd wanted to string her along, he wouldn't have backed off the way he had, would he?

On the other hand, if he just wanted to keep her off balance...

The conjecturing would make her crazy. Especially since she'd fallen in love with the man! Last weekend had absolutely brought that fact home. What was she going to do about it if she *was* Kyle's mother? What was she going to do if she *wasn't?*

Lost in her thoughts, she was surprised to hear heavy footfalls in the hallway. Her options were limited. She could either emerge from the soap bubbles and wrap a towel around herself, praying she could do that in time, or she could stay neck-deep in the soapsuds and hope Nathan wouldn't come in.

After all, why would he? He apparently didn't want more intimate contact with her.

"I'm taking a bath," she called out.

The footsteps stopped outside the door. "I'll check on Kyle," Nathan said gruffly.

"I'll dry off. I need to talk to you," Sara told him. "The doctor's office phoned."

Propriety forgotten, he stepped inside the bathroom, his gaze locking onto hers. "With the results?"

"You weren't here, and the receptionist wouldn't share them with me over the phone. I made an appointment for ten tomorrow morning, if that's okay with you. If not, I can call and change it." She stopped. "Or you can."

The bubbles were slowly disappearing and she thought she could almost hear the little pops as they did. But Nathan's gaze stayed on her face, and she wondered how much willpower that took on his part.

"Ten is fine. Was there anything else?"

She guessed he thought she'd say no. Well, bubbles or not, bathtub or not, she wasn't embarrassed by what had happened, even if he was. She had been making love, even if he hadn't been. They couldn't ignore each other for the rest of her stay. "Kyle wondered where you were tonight. I couldn't give him an answer."

"Kyle wondered?"

"I did, too," she admitted.

"I went to the Sports Den for a game of cards and a beer. It was a spur of the moment decision."

"Because you didn't want to come home?"

"Because I needed breathing space."

"Look, Nathan, I told you before, if you want me to move to the bed-and-breakfast in town—"

"Tomorrow we'll have an answer to the question that's been plaguing us. After we get that answer, we can decide what happens next. I'm going to check on Kyle and then turn in."

Before she had time to worry about another bubble popping, Nathan was gone from the bathroom and possibly gone from her life.

It all depended on those results in the morning. Everything did.

* * *

Nathan was in shock. Sara knew it, just as she knew she'd fallen in love with him and that he'd want no part of that love. That's why he'd pushed her away. Why he'd said they'd made a mistake.

He'd been silent since they'd left the doctor's office, and he kept his eyes glued to the road.

As he pulled into the driveway at his house, she leaned over and touched his arm. "Nathan, what do you want to do?"

When he turned to look at her, there was a stark desolation in his eyes, and she guessed why. He'd been holding on to the memory that Colleen was Kyle's mother. Now reality might force him to let go of that idea, and he didn't like it.

"What I want to do is go back in time a few months, before all of this started."

She tried to keep emotion from her face, but apparently she couldn't.

When he realized exactly what he'd said, he swore. "I'm sorry, Sara. This isn't your fault. It isn't anyone's fault. It just is. What I'm really having trouble adjusting to is the fact that Kyle *won't* have trouble adjusting. He's going to love the idea that you're his mother. But are you prepared for everything that follows if we tell him?"

"You mean his questions?"

"Not only his questions, but how we're going to answer them."

She'd spent most of last night thinking about what to tell Kyle. "I know he's only five and we have to put this in terms he'll understand. But we do have to tell him the truth. We can explain that he was lucky enough to have *two* mothers. He needs to know that his life won't change radically, that you're still his dad and he'll live with you, and that's the way it's going to be. When I first arrived, I told you I didn't come here to hurt anyone. Sure, I want to be involved in Kyle's life. But we're going to have to see how that might work. We can assure him we're taking one day at a time, because that's what we're doing."

She saw relief ease the lines around Nathan's eyes, and that relief almost made her sad. "What did you think I was going to do? Demand he come live with me? Don't you know me at all by now?"

Nathan rubbed his hand across his forehead. "It takes time to get to know someone, Sara. Real time. We've been in a pressured situation from the moment you stepped into the lodge. Anything you said or did was suspect, and I imagine for you, anything *I* said or did was, too. Once I'd invited you into my house, I knew I should have listened to Ben's advice and been more careful, because I realized you could watch my every move. You could be keeping a list of what I do right as a dad and what I do wrong. Now you can use that at any time, since you *are* Kyle's mother."

No wonder he thought making love had been a mistake. Not only was he still in love with his dead wife, but he was suspicious of everything Sara did. He'd been watching her, too, and she guessed he wasn't sure that she'd been genuine with him. What a pair they made.

"Do you want me to leave and not tell Kyle the truth? Do you want me to wait until he's eighteen to get to know him?"

Nathan kept his gaze on hers. "Are you saying that's what you would do if I said that was what I wanted?"

"I'm saying that *you* are Kyle's father, and that from everything I've seen, you have his best interests at heart. If you truly thought my staying out of his life was best, I'd have to consider that."

Breaking his gaze from hers, he stared straight ahead at the garage door. "Can you stay through Christmas? Kyle will be disappointed if you leave before the holiday."

She was so relieved he at least wanted her to stay that long. "I'll call my boss and arrange it. I told him I might be gone until after New Year's and he was okay with that."

After a few moments of silence, Nathan said, "I need time to think about the rest."

She wanted to ask how much time, but she didn't. Before she could plead for the chance to be a permanent part of Kyle's life, she opened the door and climbed out of the SUV.

Nathan followed her up the walk. When she glanced at him over her shoulder, she could see he was deep in thought. His eyes had a faraway look and he had his hands jammed in his pockets. He believed his life had come to a crashing halt today and would veer off in a different direction than he'd ever expected. But not because she cared about him. Not because he cared about her. Not because they'd been trying to figure out what making love had meant. But because he didn't want to share his son with a woman other than Colleen.

As soon as Sara opened the front door, her focus fell to a framed photograph sitting on one of the occasional tables. It was a picture of Nathan and Colleen dressed in snow gear. There were three pictures of the two of them in the living room—two on the bookshelves, one on that table—plus two in Kyle's bedroom and three in Nathan's. Not that Sara had been snooping. She'd simply dropped some folded laundry onto his bed one day and caught sight of them. She knew the purpose of the photographs— Nathan had wanted to assure Kyle that he'd had a mother and she'd loved him.

But now?

Would Nathan set a photograph of *her* in Kyle's room when she left?

As soon as Kyle saw Sara cross the threshold, he ran to her and wrapped his arms around her. "Sara, Sara, I got a letter. It was for me."

She crouched down to him. "Who was it from?"

She heard Nathan come in behind her, could feel his tall presence towering over her.

"It was from Uncle Ben. Val read it to me. He can't come for Christmas," Kyle said with a frown of disappointment. "He has to work on a…" He looked into the kitchen to Val.

"A trial," she said.

Kyle nodded. "He has to work on a trial. But he's sending something really special in the mail. And he said I can open it when it gets here. I don't have to wait until Christmas. Isn't that great? A present before Christmas!"

She knew about presents before Christmas. Her birthday was December 19. As a kid, she'd always loved the pre-celebration to the holiday.

"That's exciting," she agreed, realizing she had to go shopping soon, not only for Kyle, but for Nathan and Val and Galen. Then again, maybe Nathan would want her to leave. She almost wished they hadn't gotten the results yet, but she didn't want to live in limbo, either.

"Maybe it's another arrowhead," Kyle decided, sounding as if he'd be happy with that.

"Maybe. Or maybe something completely different. That's the fun of presents and surprises. You never know what you'll get or what will happen," she stated.

"What do *you* think Uncle Ben will send?" Kyle asked Nathan, obviously believing his dad knew everything.

Nathan unzipped his jacket. "Whatever he sends, I'm sure you'll like it."

"Lunch is ready," Val called from the kitchen.

After Kyle hurried to the table, Sara stood and removed her coat.

To her surprise, Nathan rezipped his jacket. "I'm going over to the lodge to see if Dad ran into anything this morning he needs help with. I'll get something in the kitchen over there."

Obviously, Nathan needed not only time to digest the test results, but space away from her. If she'd had any dreams of them being one big, happy family, they were withering fast.

Nathan waved to Kyle. "I'll see you later," he called with forced cheerfulness, and left the house.

Val cast a questioning glance at Sara.

"He has something on his mind," she told the house-keeper, while Kyle took three big gulps of milk.

"So do you," Val noted with a knowing look. "Both of you have been a little quiet since you got back after the weekend."

Although Sara felt the need to confide in Val, to seek the wisdom of her years, she didn't, for lots of reasons. Kyle's presence was definitely one of them. But she also felt as if she'd be encroaching yet again on Nathan's life if she did. Val was his friend. His dad's friend.

Thinking about Galen and Val distracted Sara for a moment. "So, did you have dinner with Galen and Kyle the day we went to Sam's cabin?"

Val looked discomfited. "Actually, I did. But…" She sighed. "Fortunately for Kyle, Galen decided we should pop a movie into the DVD player and watch it while we ate. Not that you're supposed to tell Nathan we did that, of course."

Sara smiled. "Of course. But Kyle eventually will."

"No, his Gramps told him it was a secret. He really enjoyed it, even though I had to wash ketchup off the sofa from the French fries. But it didn't give Galen and me a chance to talk at all. And I left when the movie was over. It seemed Galen had sort of expected that. I mean, why would I stay?"

To cover her self-consciousness, Val went to the table, arranged a sandwich and a few chips on Kyle's plate and gave him a smile. "Remember, you have to eat carrot sticks, too, if you eat potato chips."

Sara wandered over to the table and pulled her chair out. Conversationally, she said, "I was thinking about having my hair trimmed. Can you suggest someone in town who won't cut off a lot more than I'd like?"

"It's been years since I went to a hairdresser. My sister does mine," Val admitted, as if she'd never considered anything else. However, she cocked her head and studied Sara. "You know what? Ralph Durand from New York bought The Hair Hut. He has two hairdressers working for him. From what I understand, it takes weeks to get an appointment with him but he's really good. But I know the receptionist he hired. She's the daughter of a friend. Maybe she can get us in." The housekeeper's smile was sly, and Sara laughed.

Sara hadn't wanted to insult Val by suggesting a makeover that would shake up Galen's world a little, but the housekeeper had caught her drift. "That sounds like a great idea."

Although Val was a friend of Galen's and Nathan's, she was fast becoming a friend of Sara's, too. Circumstances changed whether Nathan wanted them to or not. He was simply going to have to get used to that idea. Somehow, she was going to convince him she needed to be in Kyle's life—and in his.

Twelve days later, Sara entered the kitchen from the garage, her arms full of packages. Not only had she finished Christmas shopping, but she'd bought herself an outfit, too. After all, it was her birthday. She hadn't told anyone because, well, she hadn't wanted Nathan to feel obliged to do anything.

However, when she stepped into the kitchen, Val, Nathan and Kyle all stared at her.

"Hi, everyone." She smiled and grabbed at a bag before it slipped to the floor.

"Why didn't you tell us it was your birthday?" Kyle asked, looking almost outraged for a five-year-old. "Val would have made you a cake."

Uh-oh. How had they found out? She hadn't said anything to anyone. She'd asked for the keys to the pickup to go into town. She'd spent time by herself, buying a silky scarf and a scented candle, calling Joanne at work over her lunch break so they could chat. Sara had phoned Joanne as soon as she'd found out she was Kyle's mother, and her friend had rejoiced with her. Sara had needed someone to be happy for her. Val and Galen weren't making their feelings known one way or the other. And Nathan...

"You got flowers and big balloons." There was awe in Kyle's voice.

"I did?"

When Kyle ran to her and clutched her arm to drag her toward the living room, she almost dropped a few more packages.

Instantly, Nathan was there beside her, gathering them. His large hand brushed hers and she felt the electric charge skitter across her skin. "Should I put these in your room?" His voice was gruff, but his expression didn't reveal what he was thinking.

"Sure. Thank you."

She couldn't miss the flowers, let alone the balloons. A dozen red roses were arranged in a crystal vase. A rainbow-colored Mylar balloon proclaiming Happy Birthday was tied to the vase, accompanied by various-colored latex ones.

"Who sent them?" Kyle asked.

"I don't know. I guess I'll have to open the card." Sara supposed Joanne could have sent them but she doubted that.

When she opened the small envelope, she was totally surprised. The note read, "Happy Birthday, kiddo. Can't wait till you get back. Ted"

She couldn't believe Ted was trying to woo her into his bed again. What had he said? *I like you, Sara. I always have. I've missed you...especially in bed. There's no reason why we can't enjoy the party circuit over the holidays together, is there?*

No way. No how.

"They're from someone at work," she told Kyle.

"He must really like you to get you a balloon *that* big."

She hadn't said they were from a man. But there was no point denying it.

"Well, I'd better be going," Val said. "Supper comes out of the oven in ten minutes. I told Galen I'd help him put up a tree at his place tonight." Crossing to Sara, Val patted her shoulder. "Happy birthday to you. Tomorrow I'm going to make you a cake. What's your favorite?"

"I love chocolate with peanut butter icing."

"That's what it'll be, then. Everyone deserves to celebrate their birthday. You should have told us. Tomorrow night I'll make something special."

"You don't have to—"

"I don't want to hear it. We're celebrating."

Ever since Val had gotten them appointments at the salon, booked for the end of the week, they'd felt like co-conspirators. Sara was growing more and more fond of the older woman.

Nathan put his hand on Kyle's shoulder. "Why don't you go finish up that project in your bedroom? I'll call you when supper's ready."

"Maybe I can finish it before we eat." Kyle gave Sara a wide, secretive smile and scurried off to his room.

Sara could feel Nathan's gaze on her. "I'd better go put away what I bought today." She started for the hall, too, but his voice stopped her. "Sara."

Slowly she turned.

"Who were the flowers from?"

"Like I told Kyle, they're from someone at work."

"A man?"

She kept quiet.

"Ted. The man you dated?"

If Nathan had any feelings for her, she wanted to know. "Why does my love life matter to you?"

"Love has nothing to do with it. But you and I…" He stopped and then shrugged. "If you're dating someone in Minneapolis and you slept with me… I just didn't think you were that type of woman."

Suddenly all the frustration, hurt and anger she'd felt

because of his attitude after they'd made love erupted. "I'll tell you the type of woman I am." She kept her voice low so Kyle couldn't hear, but it was filled with vehemence. "I'm the *type* of woman who believes in commitment. I dated Ted. I thought we had the start of something good. But then he walked away two weeks after my accident, because he learned I couldn't have children. Before I came up here, he wanted to start something up again. But not a *real* relationship. One for mutual satisfaction. And I told him I didn't know if we could even still be friends. I could never trust him again. When a man walks away once, I know he'll walk away again."

Without giving Nathan a chance to comment, she left the living room, went into her bedroom and shut the door. The realization that Nathan had the power to hurt her without even half trying hit her hard. She wished it wasn't so, but it was.

So *this* was what love felt like.

No, this was what *one-sided* love felt like. From now on she was going to concentrate on Kyle and her relationship with him. She'd always wanted to be a mother, and now she had her chance.

She wouldn't let Nathan take that away from her.

Chapter Eleven

All right, damn it! He was jealous. It had only taken Nathan a hike around the lake with ten tourists to admit it to himself. Now he had.

As the guests from the lodge thanked him, Nathan smiled and said all the right things. But inside, he was planning what he'd say to Sara. He'd hurt her last night. He'd seen the pain in her eyes. And he felt like dirt. He kept pushing her away because he wanted her close too much. He kept pushing her away because he didn't want her to take Kyle from him. Yet the morning they'd had sex at the cabin, he'd realized how much he needed her, and that didn't sit well any more than the rest.

He physically needed her. That was all.

So are you any better than Ted what's-his-name? Nathan's conscience asked him.

He didn't answer the question. He just took out his cell phone and called the house. Sara answered.

"Are you busy?" he asked.

There was a brief hesitation and her voice was cool when she replied, "I'm playing dominoes with Kyle."

"Can you come over to the lodge when you finish the game?"

He was met with silence.

"I want to show you what I got Kyle for Christmas— one of the presents that wasn't on his list," Nathan pressed.

The distance between them seemed to grow wider.

"I also want to talk to you about last night."

"All right." She finally acquiesced. "It'll probably be about fifteen minutes. Is that okay?"

"That's fine. I just returned from a hike and I want to document who went and how long we were out. Bundle up before you walk over. The wind's picking up."

"I will," she replied quietly.

At least she hadn't told him to go take another hike. Though she still might. "See you in a little while."

When Nathan hung up, he started rehearsing in his mind what he was going to say to her. It had been a long time since he'd had to apologize to a woman. Colleen used to say that *I'm sorry* were foreign words to him, words he had trouble fitting into his vocabulary. She'd been right. He hated admitting when he was wrong. Even more, he hated to admit when he'd hurt someone.

And you even did it on her birthday, his conscience reminded him.

He swore, shook his head, then went to tell his father where Sara could find him when she came to the lodge.

Twenty minutes later, Nathan was in the storeroom in the basement when Sara came down the stairs.

"Nathan," she called.

"Over here."

As she descended the last few steps, he motioned to the nearby bed. "I wanted you to see this before I took it apart. On Christmas Eve I'll set it up in the garage, and leave a note under the tree for Kyle to find it there."

As Sara's eyes moved over the twin bed, she smiled. It looked like a huge fire engine, with its wooden sides, headboard and footboard. As she came closer, she saw the ladder painted on the left, Rapid Creek Fire Company on the right.

She pointed to the dalmatian dog painted on one side of the headboard. "He's adorable."

"Do you think Kyle will like it?"

"He'll love it. Where did you get it?"

"A guy I went to high school with is a carpenter. He makes the beds and his wife paints the murals on them."

"We'll have to buy a red bedspread to go with it."

"Yes, we will," Nathan agreed.

Their gazes met and held. She was standing six feet away and not coming any closer. He remedied that by walking around the bed and approaching her, his heart beating more rapidly. "About yesterday…"

Her expression changed. It was barely perceptible, but he saw it.

"Why didn't you tell me it was your birthday?"

Apparently that wasn't what she'd expected him to say. Her shoulders relaxed a little. Just a little. "I didn't tell you because I didn't want you to feel obligated to do anything. You're the kind of man who always wants to do the right thing. I didn't want you pretending something you didn't feel."

Resting his hands on her shoulders, he gazed into her eyes. "I don't pretend when I'm around you. I can't. I feel too raw."

Her mouth rounded and he could see her surprise.

"That's why sometimes I don't say or do the tactful thing."

"Like suggesting I sleep around?" Hurt tinged her voice.

"I'm sorry, Sara. The truth is I was jealous, and knew I had no right to be. I was…disappointed you hadn't told me about your birthday. After all, with what happened at the cabin—"

"You regretted what happened."

"It wasn't regret. Our situation is a lot more complicated than that. But I shouldn't have made a judgment about you. I had no right to say anything."

"You don't want anything to change."

She was right about that. But his life *was* changing… because of *her*. She was so damn beautiful. Need coiled inside of him and he brought her closer. But when he bent his head, her hands flattened against his chest. "What do you want from me, Nathan?"

"I want to give in to the chemistry. Do you?"

"Without regrets?" Her eyes searched his.

"Without regrets."

His lips found hers, and simply the touch of mouth on mouth was like a jolt of lightning. They were sealed together by it, and the air around them sizzled. His groan was gut deep, and he pressed her to him and plunged his tongue into her mouth. She was ready for him, responded instantly, stroking against him, making him need more. Her jacket was an unwelcome barrier, and he suddenly wanted her in his bed with him, with nothing at all between them.

Suddenly footsteps sounded from above and Galen descended the steps. Before Nathan could break away from Sara, his dad saw them.

"Well, well." Galen's eyes were twinkling. "What have we here?"

For once in his life, Nathan didn't know what to say to his father. Finally he asked, "Did you want something, Dad?"

Sara stepped back, and he removed his arms from around her.

Trying to keep his amused smile in check, Galen replied, "Yeah. I need you to help me shove some furniture around on the second floor. One of the guests lost a necklace and we moved everything this morning. My back's pretty sore, so I need help pushing it back in place."

"Did she find her necklace?"

"Yes, she did. It had fallen down behind the dresser. And she checked out, so that's why there wasn't any hurry. But now there is, because Doris is going to make up the room."

"I'll be right there."

"Sara could come along and peek into the empty rooms on the third floor. You haven't seen the lodge yet, have you, Sara?"

"No, I haven't. Kyle told me about the attic, though. He thinks you have wonderful things stored there."

"There's an antique chest from way back when, filled with old clothes. Another one with old photographs. There's a tandem bike and an antique spittoon. I'm not sure why he's fascinated by all of it."

"Maybe because he senses the history behind it."

"That could be. I didn't think you were old enough to see the value in an attic full of junk." His smile was teasing.

"I have a few antiques of my mother's. I appreciate them a lot more than my new furniture."

Galen nodded, then turned back to the stairs. "I'll meet you up in room 24," he called over his shoulder.

After he'd left, Sara said, "I felt like a teenager caught on Lover's Lane."

"I know what you mean. Why is it we still feel like kids around our parents?"

"Maybe because we are. You're lucky to have your dad."

"I know I am. We have our battles, but for the most part, we are friends."

Awkwardness settled between them for a few seconds. "You don't have to look around the lodge if you don't want to."

"I'd like to see it. Can I just go on up to the third floor?"

"Yep. The six people staying up there came in a group, and they left this morning. All of the rooms have been cleaned, so you can wander in and out."

As she started up the stairs, he called, "Sara."

She turned.

"Happy birthday. We'll celebrate at dinner tonight."

The smile she gave him made him forget all about the flowers and balloons she'd received from another man. That smile made him want her as much as he did when he was kissing her.

It took Nathan about fifteen minutes to help his dad rearrange the furniture in room 24. After they'd shifted the dresser into place, Nathan was eager to hear what Sara thought of the lodge.

But Galen stopped him before he turned to go up the stairs. "Do you know what you're doing with Sara?"

Nathan met his dad's gaze. "She's Kyle's mother."

Galen didn't look surprised. "Then the question's even more important. Do you know what you're doing with her?"

"I only know I haven't felt this alive since Colleen died."

After a pensive check of Nathan's face, Galen clapped him on the shoulder. "Just take it slow and make sure it's real."

As Nathan climbed to the third floor, he knew that

nothing could be more real than Sara's kisses. Or her response in his arms.

He found her standing in the corner room, facing west. She'd removed her coat and laid it across the rose-and-blue quilted spread. This was one of the more refined rooms, with cream, flowered wallpaper and elegant maple furniture. He studied her as she stood in profile, the slanting sunlight behind her. She wore jeans and a soft pink sweater that invited him to touch it…to touch her.

"What are you looking at?" His voice was gruffer than he expected it to be.

"The beauty of the scenery. Tourists pay to get lost in it for a vacation that lasts a few days, maybe a week. You've got it all the time."

Crossing to the window, he stood beside her. "I try not to take it for granted. That's why I like hiking and cross-country skiing. It puts me in the middle of firs and lakes."

"Don't forget snowmobiling."

"I wouldn't forget snowmobiling." He slid his hands under her hair and tipped her chin up with his thumb. "I wasn't finished kissing you when we were interrupted."

"I wasn't finished kissing you, either."

The simple truth of it brought them together again, and this time no interruption was big enough to stop the kiss. The kiss overtook them and had a life of its own. It became more than Nathan ever expected, and he fought for the control to keep it in line. As his tongue explored her mouth with increasing fervor, his arms pressed her tighter to his body, until he realized he couldn't touch her the way he wanted to.

Somehow he slipped his hand between them. Somehow he found the edge of her sweater. Her skin was so warm, so soft, so Sara. His need pulsed, his heart beat faster, and thought fled in the wake of the passion between them.

Sara's breast was small and fit perfectly in his hand. She moaned and returned his kiss more ardently. There was no going back now. Though their arms and hands were tangled, she found him, cupped him, and he practically exploded. Embracing her again, he walked her to the bed and they fell onto it, only breaking their kiss when they landed, and then coming back for more.

As he ridded her of her clothes, she went to work on the buttons of his flannel shirt. While she undid them one by one, he unfastened his belt and unsnapped his jeans. He had to sit up to get rid of his boots, jeans and boxers, but it only took a few seconds. Then they were together again. While he sucked on her nipple, she stroked her fingers through his hair. The turning point came when her soft hands drifted down his chest, slid over his stomach and found him hot and hard and ready for her. He mounted her, never wanting anything as much as he wanted her at that moment…never needing anything as much. In the cabin, they'd been quick and fast and regretful. No regrets this time. They'd both agreed.

When he looked down at her, her eyes were open, gazing into his. "Tell me what you need, Sara. I want to make this good for you."

"I need you," she said simply, and the pure honesty behind her words urged him to thrust into her. He'd intended to maintain control. He'd intended to prolong their pleasure. But he soon found out pleasure had a mind of its own.

"Raise your knees," he commanded.

When she did, she received him all the way. He got lost in the satiny softness of her, the green of her eyes and the desire on her face. When she clutched his shoulders, he drove into her again and again and again. All at once he realized this was more than sex. This was losing himself. And he didn't like it at all.

Sara's orgasm brought a gasp from her, and she dug her nails into his shoulders. Her muscles contracting around him set him off, like a firecracker. He couldn't hold back. He couldn't stop it. His orgasm was off the seismic meter.

As he collapsed onto Sara, he knew he still hadn't had enough of her, and he'd want her again.

After a minute or so, he hiked himself up on his elbows and looked down at her. There were questions in her eyes.

"I don't have any answers, Sara. I just know that sex like this is rare. Whatever we've got between us isn't something I've ever experienced before."

She didn't say what she was thinking, but he could almost hear it. *What about with your wife?*

He wasn't going there now. He wasn't going to feel guilty, damn it. He was alive and Colleen was dead. He still felt married to her in so many ways. But this combustible energy between him and Sara was theirs alone.

"We need to talk about what this means to both of us," she murmured.

"No. No, we don't. Can't we just enjoy it? Can't we just go day by day and see where this leads?"

He could usually read what Sara was thinking, but right now he couldn't. Her expression was blank, and he wondered what she was hiding. Resentment because they hadn't told Kyle the truth yet? She couldn't have pretended this, could she have? Pretended desire, so she could stay close to him and close to Kyle?

Finally she said, "I don't think you're the type of man who just lives for today."

At his lack of response, she asked, "What are you thinking?"

He hiked himself away from her and sat on the edge of the bed. "Nothing that matters."

"*Everything* that matters," she countered, and clasped his shoulder. "I can practically hear your mind working. You still don't trust me, do you?"

Trust her? When she could possibly steal his son from him? "Tell me something, Sara. Have you consulted a custody lawyer yet?"

She looked guilty for a moment, but then shook her head. "No, I haven't consulted one. I do have the name of one, though."

"Just in case," he said.

"Nathan, put yourself in my shoes. What would you have done if you went to a stranger and wanted to claim paternity? I didn't know you. I didn't know how you'd react. I just wanted to be prepared."

Had he ever put himself in her shoes? Had he thought

about what the waiting around was like? First, to find out if she was Kyle's mother, and then for Nathan to make up his mind when it was time to tell Kyle? Once they told him, though, they could never take the words back. Nathan had to be sure it was the right thing to do.

"I do understand your position, Sara. I do." He didn't want tension and distrust between them. "Let's get dressed and find out what Val made for your birthday dinner," he said at last. "My guess is Kyle's so excited about it he's in her way. When I left, he was lobbying for balloons. Apparently he had some left from his own party."

Sara slid to the edge of the bed. "I want to change into something I bought yesterday."

"You're already wearing your birthday suit," he teased.

"Val would be a little shocked if I appeared like this."

"But *I* wouldn't. If you happen to wander into my room tonight, I wouldn't be shocked at all." He'd just issued an invitation if she wanted it.

He really had no clue whether she'd accept.

Tears came to Sara's eyes as Val cut her a piece of choco-late-peanut butter birthday cake. "There you go," the woman said. "And it's so good, you'll forget that Kyle made you wear that silly hat while you blew out your candles."

Sara laughed. They were all wearing silly hats, left over from Kyle's birthday. But she didn't mind. It was part of the celebration. She hadn't really celebrated her birthday since before her mother died.

Galen's pointed hat was almost falling off his head. He righted it and grinned. "Go ahead, Kyle. Give Sara your present. I helped him with it," he admitted proudly.

Sara took the large, flat package that Kyle carefully handed her. It was wrapped in Christmas paper, with a silver bow. She untied the ribbon, slipped off the paper and opened the box. Inside, she found one of Kyle's drawings framed under glass. "This is wonderful! It's you beside a fire engine, right?"

"Yep. Gramps found the frame in the attic." The frame looked as if it had seen a new coat of paint, and Sara turned to Galen, too. "Thank you, very much."

"We didn't know what color your apartment was," Galen said, "but we figured yellow would go anywhere."

Yes, it would. There were times Sara almost forgot she had a life back in Minneapolis. How could she forget about the career she'd worked so hard on? The partnership she was aiming for? But when she looked into Kyle's little face, that didn't seem to matter.

Next, Val handed her a small square package. When Sara opened it, she found a purse mirror that was beautifully beaded on the back. "This is great. Now I can always make sure my lipstick is on straight."

Val laughed and brushed away her thanks.

Finally, Nathan gave her a gift bag that held his presents. She took the sparkly bag with its snow scene and reached inside the white tissue paper. First she pulled out a gold foil box of candy—imported chocolates. "Dark chocolate is my favorite, and I love pecans." Then she pulled out the second present. It was a book, and she could see instantly that it had beautiful color pictures of the Rapid Creek area. "Oh, Nathan, I love it." And she did. When she was in Minneapolis, she'd remember fresh snow on fir trees, the lake they'd seen when they'd gone snowmobiling, the lodge itself, which was the centerpiece of one of the photographs.

"A friend of mine from high school is a photographer. The book was published last year. It's signed."

She could see that it was. She wanted to kiss Nathan. She wanted to burrow into his arms again. But with everyone sitting around the table that was impossible. Maybe tonight.

Should she really take him up on his invitation? Should she start an affair with him?

It's already started, a little voice whispered.

Yes, she guessed it was. But if she went to his bedroom tonight, she'd be telling him she wanted to live in the moment, and didn't care about the future. If she made love with him again tonight, and he didn't have deep feelings for her, she was going to take a major fall. Or…

Maybe as they were making love, Nathan's feelings would deepen and grow.

Covering her confusion, she said, "Thank you so much, everyone. You've made my birthday really special."

"A day late," Val chided.

"This belated birthday is the best one I've had in a long time."

Galen picked up his fork to dig into his cake. He commented, "And Christmas is right around the corner. Then we'll *all* have presents to open. If we've been good," he added, with a conspiratorial glance at Kyle.

"Will Santa bring Sara's presents here or leave them at her house?" The boy looked worried that she wouldn't have anything to open.

"Oh, I think Santa will know she's here," Nathan assured him.

She might have Christmas presents here, but the day after New Year's she'd be leaving. Unless Nathan asked her to stay. Unless she decided to change her life to be near her son.

After Nathan and Sara put Kyle to bed, they wandered into the living room, both of them acting a little awkward. Nathan said, "It takes him awhile to get settled in and fall asleep sometimes. The snow has stopped. I'm going to go out and run the blower on the walks."

She didn't know what to say to that. It sounded as if he was expecting her to come to his room. If she didn't, would he be angry?

As if sensing her turmoil, he took her hand and kissed her fingertips one by one. "I want you to come to my room tonight. But if that's not what you want, I'm not going to act like an idiot, either. We're adults, Sara. We each have to make our own decisions."

If she told him she loved him, she knew he'd back away. She knew he'd retreat. Love and sex were separate for him. Apparently, he could shut down his memories of Colleen while he met a physical need with Sara. On the other hand, if she showed him she loved him, over and over again, in every way she could, maybe he'd come to believe. Maybe then he could let go of the past to reach for a future. "I'll be waiting for you when you come back in."

He actually grinned at her, a full-fledged smile. Giving her a hug, he assured her, "I'll make this fast."

After Nathan went outside, Sara took a bubble bath, then listened for the snowblower to stop humming. She was in the kitchen, trying to control the runaway beat of her pulse, when he came in. His cheeks were ruddy, his hair windswept, and he looked too delicious for words.

"Would you like a mug of hot chocolate? I can bring it to the bedroom."

"I'm going to grab a five-minute shower. I'll meet you there."

By the time she stirred the mix into the milk and carried it to his bedroom, the water had stopped running. When he came out of the bathroom, he was naked, and she was filled with an excitement that made her breathless.

She didn't know why she'd fallen so hard and fast for Nathan. She didn't know why, the moment they'd met, her heart rate had sped up and her skin had tingled. There was something about him that unsettled her, excited her and made her feel every inch a woman. She also knew with that deep feminine instinct she often depended on that he would make a wonderful life partner—loyal, faithful and dependable. If he could bundle up the past and open up the gifts she wanted to give him in the present, they could have a future together.

As he came to the bed, slid in beside her and turned to her, she went willingly into his arms. They held each other for long moments of quiet intimacy, moments so fantastic that tears burned in her eyes. He was still slightly damp from his shower, smelled like soap and man, and heated her body with his. She felt him grow hard with his need for her.

She wanted to crawl into him, letting her mind and heart, soul and body join his.

"I can't believe I'm hungry for you again," he growled into her neck, nipping the tender skin under her ear, passing his hand down her side and then between her legs. Already, the touch of his fingers on her skin was enough to make her thoughts scatter like a drift of snow blown by the wind.

When he took his hand from her most intimate place, she gazed up at him, wondering if he'd decided this wasn't what he wanted, after all.

"This afternoon was too fast. We hardly had time to catch our breath, let alone enjoy what we were doing. Instead of rushing toward the big bang, I thought you might enjoy a lot of little bangs." He softly kissed her mouth, nibbled at the corner, titillated her with kisses from her jaw down her neck to her breasts.

Although the pleasure he was bestowing on her had her almost dizzy, she reached for him, determined to make him as crazy as he was making her. She stroked her palm down his back, dawdled at the small of it and felt him grow harder.

When her fingertips reached across his buttocks, he swore. "You keep that up and we'll be done."

"But there's always the next time," she breathed against his cheek, giving him a kiss there, too.

The next time with him was all she could hope for. But eventually their next times were going to run out.

She couldn't think about that now. She couldn't think about leaving—either Kyle *or* Nathan.

He rolled onto his back, to keep her fingers from wandering farther. But he brought her with him, and they laughed as she balanced herself on his chest and legs, then sat up, boldly stroking his pectoral muscles.

"I thought it would be better this way," he breathed raggedly. "But your hands are lethal."

"No more lethal than your mouth."

He grinned at her. With his hair falling over his brow, he looked more relaxed, more happy than she'd ever seen him. If she could do that for him, wouldn't he want her in his life?

"Are you ready?" she teased, tracing circles with her thumbs on his stomach, seeing his eyes darken, watching the hunger flare.

"Are *you* ready?" he asked, turning the tables on her. "Because I can hold out long enough to give you more than one orgasm."

"Is that your goal?"

"My goal is to make us both love what we're doing here."

Love. If she said it now…

When she slid back farther on his thighs, he grabbed her arms. "Where are you going?"

"You'll see."

With that pronouncement, she bent to him, let her hair trail across his stomach, her lips nuzzle his navel. He groaned her name. It was a plea. A warning. A protest. With uninhibited sureness, letting her love guide her because she'd never done anything like this before, she gently rubbed her cheek against his arousal. He went perfectly still, as if he was trying to control every muscle in his body and every thought in his head.

She nuzzled him, kissed him, then teased him with her tongue.

His hands moved restlessly against the sheet. When she took him into her mouth, she heard him sigh and she felt his heat. She knew she was being provocative and tempting, and anything but passive.

Awkwardly, his hands grasped her arm. "Enough," he rasped. "Slide onto me. Now."

"But I thought—" she began innocently.

"Dammit, Sara, *now.*"

She couldn't hide her smile or her satisfaction as she guided him into her body and sank onto him. She didn't care about multiple orgasms. She only cared about loving Nathan.

While her body hugged him, he plunged deeper. She took him in completely, finding her rhythm with him.

Mindful not only of his own pleasure, but hers, too, he reached between them, touched her, and she felt herself flying into a thousand pieces. She was trying to regain her breath, trying to concentrate on *him,* when he touched her again, stunning her with an overload of erotic sensation.

He kept their rhythm, and each ripple of pleasure turned into another until he climaxed, too. His deep, guttural groan told her he'd been as satisfied as she was.

When his body finally relaxed, she leaned forward and kissed his lips. He smiled and took her into his arms. They rolled onto their sides, holding each other close.

Sara didn't know what time it was when Kyle awakened them. He ran into his dad's room saying, "Daddy, Daddy, I can't find Sara. She's not in her room—" And then he saw the two of them together in the big bed.

She was naked under the covers, and wasn't sure what to do.

Nathan sat up, slipped on jogging shorts that were by the side of the bed, and went to his son. "What's the matter? Did you have a bad dream?"

"No. I just wanted to tell Sara something."

Nathan hunkered down beside him. "What did you want to tell her?"

Kyle looked over at her with his little-boy smile. "I'm going to write Santa a letter tomorrow and tell him you're here," he declared. "Then he'll know to leave your presents. I want you to have presents to open on Christmas morning."

"Why don't we go to your room and talk about it?" Nathan suggested.

"I don't have to go to sleep right away?"

"Sara and I have something to tell you before you do."

Nathan's gaze met Sara's, and she knew the moment

had come. Her hands trembled as she heard their voices move down the hall. She donned her nightgown and robe.

When she entered Kyle's room, he was sitting on his bed, his legs dangling. Nathan sat on one side of him and she perched on the other.

"What do you want to tell me?" Kyle asked, sounding a bit worried. "Is it about Santa?"

"No, it's about *Sara*," Nathan said with a smile. "We have a story to tell you."

Sara let Nathan take the lead, because he knew how much Kyle could comprehend.

"When your mom and I got married we wanted to have children very much. But after a while we found out we couldn't. A baby had to come from one of your mom's eggs, but we found out she didn't have good eggs. So Sara gave your mom one of *her* eggs. The doctor put it inside your mom, and you grew inside her belly. Remember those pictures I showed you, when her tummy was really big?"

"Yeah. You said I was in there, and then I came out."

"And then you came out."

Sara knew Nathan was remembering everything. The procedures for Colleen to become pregnant, the joy when she did, the misery, grief and loss, over her and Kyle's twin. Maybe this was one of the reasons Nathan *hadn't* been ready to tell his son—because all of it would come rushing back.

"The thing is, Kyle..." Nathan draped his arm around the child's shoulders. "Colleen was your mom because you grew inside of her. But Sara's your mom, too, because it was her egg that gave you life, that made you the little boy you are."

Shifting away from his dad, Kyle crawled up onto his knees and hugged Sara around the neck. She wrapped her arms around him and held him tightly, letting her tears fall.

"Why are you crying?" he asked when he pulled away and saw them.

"Because I'm so happy. I'm so glad you're my son."

"Are you going to live here with us?"

Nathan broke in, his voice rough. "She can't do that, Kyle. She has a job in Minneapolis. But she's going to visit often."

Nathan hadn't hesitated one bit. He hadn't even looked at her for confirmation. And in *his* mind it was all settled. In his mind, he was the dad. He was still the single parent. She would live 120 miles away and visit when it was convenient for him.

"I have a book I've been saving for you that can answer more questions if you think of any. Now it's time to go to sleep again." Nathan patted the pillow. "Come on, let's get you tucked in."

Kyle's gaze lifted to Sara again. "I'm glad you're my mom. But I wish you could stay here."

"So do I," she answered. "But I'll visit often. We'll talk about it more in the morning." She leaned down and kissed his forehead. "Good night, honey."

His eyes on hers, he smiled. "Can I call you Mom?"

With a lump in her throat the size of Minnesota, Sara nodded.

Once Nathan had joined her in the hall, she said, "You explained it to him in terms he could understand."

Nathan ran his hand through his hair. "I tried. I'm sure he'll have more questions. Some of them might not be so easy to answer."

As they walked down the hall, Nathan didn't put his arm around her. He didn't take her hand or invite her into his room. He looked like a man who was wrestling with the past.

"Telling Kyle reminded you of everything that happened," she said softly.

"Yeah. It did."

Just a few hours ago she'd been touching Nathan intimately, and he'd been touching her. Now she could see he didn't want to be touched. He didn't want to be consoled. He wanted to be left alone with his memories.

At the door to her bedroom, she stopped. "I never imagined we'd tell him tonight."

"It was time."

"Nathan—"

When she would have clasped his arm, he moved away. "Let's just let everything settle down a bit."

"All right. Do you still want me to help you decorate the church in the morning?"

He forced a smile. "Sure."

They didn't have anything else to say. She stepped into her room. "Good night."

He studied her for several heartbeats. "Good night, Sara."

As she sat down on her bed, she heard his door close. She was afraid another door had closed tonight, too—the door to his heart.

Chapter Twelve

The tension between Sara and Nathan was as reverberating as the church bell that rang at noon. She felt his gaze on her as she arranged straw on the floor of the wooden stable he'd carried to the front of the church. They'd assembled it in silence, and now she had to do something to break that silence.

"Do you do this every year?"

"Dad used to do it, and his father before him." Nathan's voice was low, filled with memories.

"My mother and I usually made pine bough wreaths with red velvet bows to hang around the church. We'd make them a few evenings before Christmas, so the scent of the pine was still fresh."

After a few moments, Nathan added, "Dad brought us to the midnight service on Christmas Eve. He knew we'd be awake anyway, so he insisted we might as well be doing something worthwhile, remembering what Christmas was really about."

"There's something special about that midnight service, isn't there? When I was little, my mom would tell me if I listened hard enough I could hear the angels sing. I think I still listen for them. Will you…will we bring Kyle to the midnight service?"

"I'd like to, but with the temperature dropping after sundown, it will be better to wait until the eleven o'clock service on Christmas morning."

Sara was concerned. Kyle missed so many special events because of his asthma. Or maybe not so much because of his asthma, but because of Nathan's protective attitude about it. Now wasn't the time to bring that up, though.

After readjusting the manger between the statues of Mary and Joseph, Sara arranged straw around it.

"He's thrilled you're his mother."

"And you wish he wasn't."

"That's not true."

Their gazes locked and she saw the turmoil in Nathan's. "What are you most concerned about? That I'll want to visit him too much? That I'll interfere in your life? That I'll want to take Kyle back to Minneapolis with me?"

At that his eyes narrowed. "I wouldn't let that happen."

She didn't want to fight with him. She didn't want a tug-of-war about whether a little boy needed his mom or his dad more. She certainly didn't want to dwell on the legal question of which of them might have more rights to Kyle, because she knew she'd lose. Nathan had raised him. They were attached the way a father and son should be.

"I can't just bow out of your life and pretend I don't have a connection to Kyle."

Approaching her, he towered over her as she knelt at the manger, preparing it for the baby who would lie in it on Christmas Eve. When Nathan clasped her shoulder, she felt real compassion emanating from him. "I know this isn't easy for either of us. Telling Kyle last night really threw me."

Was it telling Kyle that had thrown him? Or had the emotions they'd stirred up in bed done so? Some thought to be having here in church! Yet as her glance strayed to the wooden pulpit, to the dais, Sara could so easily picture her and Nathan being married here.

Married. Did she think being married was a solution to this? It was one Nathan wouldn't even consider…because he wouldn't admit he had feelings for her.

When she rose to her feet, she'd never been more aware of Nathan as a man, of what he meant to her and could always mean to her. In the hollow stillness of the empty church, she sent up a prayer for direction, one straight from her heart. Would it be answered?

Yet she didn't need a divine voice to tell her Kyle should come first, no matter what it cost her, no matter what she had to sacrifice.

Sara and Nathan were so focused on each other that they didn't hear the side door of the church open. She was aware that someone else had come in only when the door banged shut and a short, stout woman with frizzy gray hair untied the red scarf around her neck and stomped over to where they were working.

Nathan reacted first. "Hello, Mrs. Evanston." Observing the flakes of snow on her quilted green coat, he asked, "It's snowing again?"

"Sure is. This is one part of the country that doesn't have to worry about a white Christmas. We get one every year."

"Sara, this is Mrs. Evanston. She and Val are in a quilting circle together."

Sara took that to mean that this woman and Val were friends, and she extended her hand. "Hello. It's good to meet you. I'm Sara Hobart."

"Yes, I know." Mrs. Evanston's gray brows arched. "I've heard lots of rumors about you."

"Not from Val," Nathan assured Sara in a firm tone.

"No, not from Val. She won't confirm or deny anything I ask her. And I don't know why. It's better that the truth be known. I heard that you all had DNA samples done or something. I thought they only used that to solve crimes. But then someone explained to me that labs use them to figure out who the mom of a child could be, or the dad." The woman's brown eyes targeted Sara. "We all know Nathan is Kyle's father. No doubt about that. The boy looks just like him."

"Mrs. Evanston, this really isn't anyone's business but ours."

Sara could tell Nathan was attempting to be patient, trying not to say something he shouldn't, or anything that would harm Val's friendship with the woman. If she had one.

"That's not true, boy, and you know it. Like someone said, it takes a village. When you came back here to live, everyone knew how tough the going was for you. We all knew you and your wife had trouble having kids, and Kyle was one of those in vitro babies, even though Colleen carried him."

"Mrs. Evanston…" Nathan's voice held a warning tone now.

"So just to put any talk to rest—"

"There shouldn't *be* any talk, Mrs. Evanston." He gave the woman a very forced smile. "Sara is our houseguest and Kyle is very fond of her. That's all anybody needs to know. Now why don't you tell me what we can help you with, why you came in here, and we can finish decorating."

The woman's eyes narrowed, but it must have been obvious to her that Nathan wasn't going to say more. Or if he did, she wouldn't like what he had to say. Mrs. Evanston switched her attention to Sara. "You're staying through the New Year?"

To forestall a quick response from Nathan, Sara simply replied, "I'm going to enjoy the holidays with the Barclay family." She motioned to the stack of evergreen boughs on the floor. "I suppose you came in for these. Would you like me to help you carry some to the parsonage?"

Seeing that Sara was giving her an out, probably also hoping she could wheedle more information on the walk over to the house, the older woman nodded. "I'd appreciate that. If I carry too many, I'm afraid I'll slip and fall."

Sara didn't look at Nathan as she put on her coat, gathered up some pine and helped the woman carry it outside.

Fifteen minutes later, Sara returned to the church and found Nathan tying the remaining boughs into a bundle. The manger scene was as complete as it would be until Christmas Eve. He had positioned the donkey and the ox near Joseph and Mary, and hung the angel on the peak of the small stable.

Picking up the ladder, he informed her, "I'm going to return this to Reverend Weiglehoff's garage."

When he would have brushed past her, Sara stepped into his path. "Are you going to tell anyone in Rapid Creek that I *am* Kyle's mother? Or are you going to wait until I leave and hope no one thinks about it anymore or asks questions?"

He propped the ladder upright, next to his booted foot. "What did you want me to say to her, Sara? She's a gossip. She's one of Val's least favorite people. If I had told her anything, anything at all, it would have gotten twisted and turned until even *you* wouldn't recognize the truth."

"I *know* the truth. It would have been very simple to say, 'Yes, Sara Hobart is Kyle's mother. Isn't science wonderful? She enabled me and my wife to have a baby, and now I'm acknowledging that fact. Kyle knows about it and is pleased.'"

"This is my private business."

"It's *our* business."

The wind whistled against the stained glass windows, rattling a loose pane. "I want to tell the whole world, Nathan, and you don't want to tell anyone. I'm not sure where we can find a compromise in that. Are you embarrassed by the way Kyle was conceived?"

"No."

"But you'd like to deny it. You'd like to believe Colleen was the only mother he ever had and the only mother he'll *ever* have."

Although Nathan was silent, that silence was louder than any "yes" he could say. And it hurt her more than harsh words ever could. "I'll tell Reverend Weiglehoff we're finished here, then I'll wait for you in the truck," he finally murmured.

Nathan didn't stop her from leaving the church. He didn't see the tears that came as she stumbled into the cold air and took great big lungfuls of it. He didn't call her name to tell her she was all wrong about what she thought.

Because she wasn't wrong. He loved his dead wife. And Sara couldn't compete with a ghost that powerful.

Kyle rushed into the kitchen the morning before Christmas and threw his arms around Sara. "Dad said we're gonna do something special tonight for Christmas Eve. What are we gonna do?"

Although Sara stooped to hug her son, and all of her attention was on him for those few moments, she was aware of Nathan a few feet away. After breathing in his little-boy pajama scent, she rose to her feet again. "I'm not sure what your dad has in mind."

If that wasn't the understatement of the year. They'd been keeping their distance, wary of what the other was going to say or do next. Kyle was a touchy subject, yet what else was as important to them both? Their own relationship...

They didn't seem to have one where Nathan was concerned.

"I thought we'd start a tradition, something we could do every year," Nathan suggested.

A tradition that included her? She wouldn't ask him that in front of Kyle. "What's your favorite meal?" she asked her little boy, wondering how she was ever going to leave him.

"Hot dogs and baked beans."

She laughed. "Okay. Well, maybe we could start out the evening with supper, cooking hot dogs and baked beans. We could ask Gramps and Val to join us. Afterward maybe we could light that big red candle over there, sing Christmas carols and then read the Christmas story."

Kyle's eyes were shining. "I want to sing 'Jingle Bells' and 'Silent Night.'"

"Everybody probably knows those two. Good choices."

Her gaze finally met Nathan's. "Are you busy this afternoon...before supper, I mean?"

"What did you have in mind?" The look in his eyes told her he wasn't thinking about what *she* had in mind. But being intimate with Nathan again was out of the question until she knew he could trust her. Until she knew she meant more than a physical release.

"I saw the ice cream maker when I went to the basement for the potatoes. With all that snow out there, I thought we could make ice cream for dessert."

"Ice cream! Ice cream!" Kyle chanted gleefully.

"But it would also mean a trip to the store. I'll need whipping cream as well as the hot dogs and baked beans," Sara informed them.

"I'll give Dad a break this afternoon and he can take you to the store. He's also more adept at making ice cream. That was his machine."

In other words, Nathan wasn't going to spend any more time with her than he had to. Tonight was an exception because of Kyle and the holiday.

All at once, Kyle ran to the phone. "I'm going to call Gramps and ask him to come for supper." Kyle pressed the speed-dial button for his grandfather and waited.

Nathan studied Sara for a long moment. "Are you trying to make a match between Val and Dad?"

"I think the match is already made. They just don't know it. Or rather, your dad doesn't know it." Yesterday she'd gone with Val to the beauty salon, where they'd both had their hair cut. Sara kept her usual style. Val, however, dispensed with her bun. Now permed, her hair fell in soft, attractive waves around her face.

"They've been spending more time together," Nathan mused.

"Do you have a problem with that?"

"No, of course not. I want to see Dad happy. But I don't think we should meddle."

"If you think inviting Val to Christmas Eve dinner is meddling, then you don't have to invite her. It was just a suggestion."

"Sara—" He sounded frustrated.

She certainly knew the feeling. Whatever he was going to say was lost when Kyle said loudly and enthusiastically into the phone, "Gramps, we want you to come for hot dogs. We're going to sing carols and everything."

When Sara would have stepped away to finish preparing breakfast, Nathan caught her arm. His fingers scorched her skin. The air around them crackled. Their gazes held and she felt the world stand still. Then Nathan broke the intensely intimate moment.

When he released her, he muttered, "If Kyle wants to call Val, too, that's fine. But she might be hard to get on her day off."

"She bought a cell phone yesterday. I have the number."

"Val? A cell phone?"

"She decided it was a good idea. Then even if she was out shopping, your dad could reach her."

Nathan simply shook his head and crossed to the door. "We're getting a few guests at the lodge this morning. I have to make sure everything is ready." When he'd shrugged into his coat, he added, "We'll have to remember to call Ben after supper tonight."

"Is he spending the holiday alone?"

"With his work. That's how he spends most of his time. I'm just glad he got here at Thanksgiving."

"Do you think Sam might change his mind and come home?"

"I wish he would. But Sam is stubborn. And…" Nathan lowered his voice "…it's hard for him to be around Kyle, knowing he could have had a child of his own. Christmas is about kids. He went to the cabin so he didn't have to deal with children at the clinic, children on TV, children in the stores."

As if he'd said too much, Nathan frowned. Zipping his parka, he went to Kyle, kissed his forehead and ruffled his hair while he was still talking to Galen. But without a goodbye to her, Nathan left for the lodge. Soon she'd be saying goodbye to him, not knowing how long it would be until she saw him again.

Soon she'd be saying goodbye, not knowing if he cared.

Sara understood the true meaning of Christmas this year. On Christmas Day, as she sat beside Galen on the sofa, watching *It's a Wonderful Life,* Kyle played with his new toys on the floor. Nathan pretended to be watching the old movie, his mind obviously elsewhere.

When the phone rang, he heaved himself out of the chair and went to the kitchen for it. "Sam! Are you in town?"

Kyle ran to his father. "Is it Uncle Sam? Can I talk to him?"

After a few moments, Nathan handed over the phone. "He said he couldn't let the holiday go by without wishing you a Merry Christmas."

"I knew my boy wasn't so selfish he wouldn't even say Merry Christmas," Galen muttered.

Kyle and Sam talked for a while, then Kyle handed his dad the phone and ran back to the living room to tell everyone about his conversation. "He drove a long way away so he could use his cell phone. He said Patches wishes us a Merry Christmas, too. But he doesn't know when he's coming back."

Galen went into the kitchen and took the phone, and soon Nathan was lowering himself into the easy chair once more.

"Why doesn't he know when he's coming back, Dad?" Kyle asked.

"He has some thinking to do, as well as ice fishing. But I bet he'll be back in a few more weeks, when the holidays are over."

Galen returned to the living room and sank down beside Sara. "I just wish he'd get over Alicia and get back to his life."

"He's over Alicia. What he isn't over is his poor judgment in choosing her. Or what she did," Nathan stated.

Kyle eyed the dinosaur figures under the tree that Ben had sent, but then reached for the set of vehicles Sara had bought him. He removed the bus, then the truck, then the airplane. After he zoomed the little plane around for a bit, he announced, "I'm gonna fly in an airplane to go see…Mom." Swiveling toward Sara, he gave her a grin.

Tears came to her eyes at Kyle's use of the coveted title, and she felt put on the spot. Both Nathan and Galen were looking at her and she wasn't sure how to handle this. They might think she'd prompted Kyle, but she hadn't. On the other hand, she wanted to keep the possibility of his visit open as an option. "We'll have to see what we can do about that."

The expression on Nathan's face told her they'd be talking about this later.

"Later" came when Kyle was trying to find a place for his new toys in his room. She'd gone to her bedroom to put away Galen's present—a pair of leather, fur-lined gloves. She fingered the jasper bracelet Nathan had given her. It was the one she'd admired in a catalog.

As she was tucking the gloves into a drawer, Nathan pushed open her door and leaned casually against the dresser, although his expression was anything but casual. "Did you tell Kyle he could fly to Minneapolis to see you?"

She closed the drawer, knowing she'd need her full attention for this discussion. "No, I didn't. But it's not such a far-fetched idea. Maybe he could visit me in the summer. I could fly up here and take him back with me."

"Absolutely not. He's only five. And you don't know how to protect him," Nathan said.

"Maybe he doesn't need as much protection as you think." The subject had been simmering under the surface for a long time. She hadn't expressed her opinion about it, but now maybe she should.

As if Nathan had been ready for an argument, he asked, "What's that supposed to mean?"

"It means you have a little boy who should experience the world outside of this house. He must feel like a prisoner sometimes."

Nathan's eyes grew even stormier, but she went on anyway. "I know he has asthma. I know that's not a condition to be taken lightly. But Nathan, he's a *child*. He needs interaction with other children. Hiring a tutor for him is the last thing you should do. He's already isolated. He needs to go to kindergarten, play, color and learn with other kids."

"And what happens if he has an attack while he's at school?"

"There are trained professionals there to deal with that."

"What happens if he has an attack when he's with *you?*"

"I've already read everything I can about asthma. I'll have his medicines, his inhalers. I can call an ambulance, take him to the hospital—"

"And what happens if that ambulance is just three minutes too late?"

She sighed. "You are *so* inflexible. You can't see that Kyle having a mother, a living mother, is as important as him having a father. You can't see that his emotional health is as important as his physical health. You and Galen and Val just aren't enough. If I thought for a minute you'd hop on a plane with Kyle and come to see me for more than a couple of days, I wouldn't push—"

Nathan held up his hand. "What was that?"

She'd been on a roll and hadn't heard a thing. "What was what?"

"It sounded like the door. Kyle wouldn't go out," Nathan muttered. "It's too cold. It's too dark." He was already on his way to Kyle's room, then to the guest room, then to the main part of the house. But his son was nowhere to be found. When Nathan grabbed his jacket, Sara reached for her coat and followed him to the door.

Outside, she ran to keep up with him. "Do you think he went to your dad's?" she asked breathlessly, as the cold air pierced her lungs and the wind whipped around her.

"I pray that he did. Anyplace else could be lethal. It's below freezing and…"

At the lodge, Nathan pulled open the door and hurried inside. He took the stairs two at a time until he got to his father's door. It was standing open.

Sara heard crying. Kyle was with Galen, and she let out a breath of relief.

However, once inside Galen's apartment, she began to worry all over again. Tears were running down Kyle's face and he was hiccuping. When he saw her, he ran to her and hugged her. "I want you to stay. I want you to live with us."

Sara crouched down and rubbed Kyle's back. He was shivering because he'd been outside without a coat. "Honey, I can't live with you. I told you that. I have a job in Minneapolis."

"If you can't live with us, then I wanna visit you." He looked up at Nathan. "Why don't you want me to go see her? Why can't we both go?" The words ended on a sob and Kyle began to wheeze. His face lost its color.

Nathan pulled an inhaler from his pocket, separated Kyle from Sara and held it to the boy's lips.

Kyle knew what he had to do. He sucked it in, coughed, and then breathed it in again. As Sara studied him, she could see him relaxing, could see he was breathing more normally.

With his arm around Kyle, Nathan assured him, "We'll talk about visiting with Sara. We will. I promise."

Kyle laid his head against his dad's shoulder, believing him.

Nathan asked Galen, "Do you have a spare blanket I can wrap him in? We'll let him calm down, then I'll go get the truck and heat it up."

The color was coming back in Kyle's face now and he wasn't wheezing anymore.

The immensity of what had just happened shook Sara to her foundation. Seeing Kyle's color fade, blue tinge his lips...

All at once, she knew Nathan had been right. He wasn't being inflexible, he was being a father. What *would* she have done if this had happened with her? Would she have reacted so swiftly? Would she have had his inhaler in her pocket? Would Kyle's health be safe in her hands?

Tonight would never have happened if Kyle didn't already feel torn between the two of them.

She knew what she had to do, for all their sakes. She had to go back to Minneapolis and possibly not return for a very long time.

Chapter Thirteen

Sara's one big suitcase was packed and ready. Her computer travel bag was zipped. She silently carried them both to the door and set them on the floor. Her throat tightened with a pain that would never go away.

Knowing she had to leave before she changed her mind, she soundlessly walked to Kyle's room and pushed open the half-closed door. If he was asleep, she wasn't going to awaken him. She'd send him a letter and explain as best she could. At least that was her plan.

However, her plan changed when she bent to kiss Kyle's forehead and his eyes opened. "Mom," he murmured, pushing himself up on his elbows and blinking the sleep from his eyes. "Did you have a bad dream?" he asked.

She smiled, though emotion caught in her throat. She swallowed it, knowing Kyle's security and happiness had to come before all else. "No, I didn't have a bad dream. I came in to tell you…that I'm leaving, honey."

When he would have protested, she hurried on. "I'm so glad I'm your mom, because you're the most special boy in the whole world. I wish I could stay, but I don't think that's the best thing for you. You belong with your dad. He knows what's good for you and he knows how to take care of you. In a few months, maybe around Easter, I'll visit again, because I want to see how much you've grown and how much you've learned. I promise I'll write to you. And you can write to me about absolutely anything you want, as often as you want. You can tell me about Val and Gramps, who your friends are and what you're doing. When you're much, much older, then maybe you can visit me."

Kyle's baseball night-light sent a mellow glow through the room. In the shadows, she could see him studying her, weighing her words, realizing the intent in them. "How old do I have to be to visit you? Sixteen?"

To Kyle, sixteen was very, very old.

"That sounds like a good age," she agreed. "You'd be old enough to fly on your own."

"You can't stay because of your job," he mumbled.

"I can't stay for lots of reasons. But mostly I can't stay because I want what's best for you."

"Will you write me a letter as soon as you get home?"

"I will. I'll tell you all about my plane ride."

"Are you leaving now?"

"Yes."

"Are you going to tell Dad?"

"I wrote him a letter. He'll find it when he wakes up."

After he thought about that, Kyle asked, "Can you stay till I fall asleep?"

"Sure I can. Move over and I'll sit here on the bed beside you."

He waited until she was next to him, then he wrapped his arms around her neck. "I love you."

"I love you, too." The ache in her chest made swallowing difficult. "Come on now, let's get you tucked in." She pulled the covers up to his chin, but Kyle extricated one arm and held her hand. Ten minutes later his breathing was even, his little face peaceful, his sleep deep.

Leaving was the hardest thing she'd ever have to do. She so wanted to stay. She wanted to move her life here. She not only loved Kyle, she loved his father. But Nathan wasn't ready for that love.

Stroking Kyle's hair from his brow, she blinked several times. Then she rose from his bed, hesitated in the doorway a long time, just staring at him, then left his room and stood in the hall outside of Nathan's door.

She knew they had nothing to say to each other, nothing more to share. Her presence would cause a wedge between father and son. She would never do anything to damage the bonds Nathan had formed with Kyle. They were too important and too necessary.

Pulling the letter she'd written to Nathan from her pocket,

she slid it under his door. She couldn't bear a goodbye scene with him. She was afraid he would be glad to see her go, and she couldn't stand to see that relief in his eyes. She didn't want to believe that she meant nothing to him.

Stopping for her purse in her bedroom, she glanced around the room, then quickly left it. She hoped Galen would understand why she had to leave like this. She hoped he would give her a ride to the airport. In a few hours, she'd be on the first flight out to Minneapolis…her home.

When Nathan awakened, light was just breaking through the clouds outside of his window. Christmas Day came rushing back, especially Christmas night. After he'd gone to bed, he'd had difficulty falling asleep, thinking about everything that had happened—what he'd said, what Sara had said, the expression on her face when Kyle couldn't breathe.

They had to talk. He rose quickly, then stopped cold when he saw the envelope on the carpet inside his door.

Going still, he listened for a moment, and detected a peculiar emptiness about the house. Sara wouldn't have taken Kyle—

With the letter in hand, he ran to his son's room and pushed open the door.

To his relief, Kyle was sleeping peacefully, lying on his side, his hand tucked under his cheek.

With a foreboding he didn't want to face, Nathan went to Sara's room, knowing what he'd find. There was no trace of her. It was empty.

Slipping her letter from its envelope, he read it swiftly.

Nathan—

I thought leaving like this was the best way. I'll be writing to Kyle as soon as I get back and I hope you will give him my letters. I'm not going to abandon him, no matter what is or isn't happening between the two of us. He's my son. He knows that. I wish I could be with him every day. But I saw last night I could harm the relationship the two of you have, and even Kyle's health. I won't do that. In a few weeks maybe we can talk about when I can visit again. I thought Easter might be a good time. I understand you want to keep your life separate from mine, even though concerns about Kyle might tie us together. I wish we could have had more, not for Kyle's sake, but for ours. But you're not ready to accept another woman in your life.

Take care. Give my love and a hug to Kyle.

Sara

She was gone. She thought that was best. Wasn't her leaving the solution he wanted? Wasn't he relieved?

The emptiness he felt in the pit of his soul was *not* relief.

Three days later Nathan had returned from a day of ice fishing and was stowing gear in one of the outbuildings when Galen stepped inside. He was frowning.

"Problem?" Nathan asked.

"Yeah, a big one. *You.* Bert said you were a great ice fishing guide but a lousy conversationalist. He returns here every year because he likes our lodge and *our* company. I don't want to lose business because you can't get your personal life straightened out."

Ever since Sara had left, Nathan had felt as if he'd lost something important. *He'd* lost it, not Kyle. He'd lost Sara.

"There's nothing to straighten out," he grumbled.

"The hell there isn't! You know, when your mother left—and yes, I still remember that day—I knew there was no hope in getting her back. She didn't want to be here. She wanted a life I couldn't give her, a career she'd always dreamed of and a man she left behind. But Sara...Sara didn't *want* to leave. You drove her away."

"I did no such thing!"

"You made her feel as though she wasn't qualified to be Kyle's mother because she hadn't lived with him for the past five years and dealt with his asthma. You made her feel as if you, and only you, could care for her son. *Her* son. He's hers, too. He needs a live mother, boy, not a *dead* one."

Nathan kept silent, more than a little annoyed with his father for being so blunt.

"You're thinking you have to keep Colleen's memory alive for Kyle or he'll never know her. You're thinking you loved her and that love was important, and you can't bear the thought of it dwindling into nothing. You're thinking

Colleen was the most important person in your life and you can't love someone else because that means you'd be forgetting about *her.*"

Nathan's chest tightened and ached because his father had gotten so close to the truth. Colleen had been his first real love. She'd known how much he'd wanted children, and she'd done everything in her power to give him babies. She'd even died.

His throat practically closed, but he managed to say, "When Colleen and I were having so much trouble getting pregnant—" He stopped. "She told me we didn't have to have children to have a long happy marriage…that the two of us were enough. But I pushed. I wanted kids. So she went along…and she died."

Galen was shaking his head. "So *that's* the guilt you've been carrying. *That's* what won't let you move on." He clasped Nathan's shoulder. "When two people marry for the right reasons, they want to do everything in their power to make the other person happy. But I know for a fact, Nathan, Colleen wanted children, too. She told me that more than once. She had a mind of her own. She wouldn't have kept trying with such joy and excitement if she hadn't wanted babies as much as you. Let it go, son. Let *her* go."

Nathan looked away from his dad. "You make it sound so easy."

"It might be easy if you'd realize what you've got. Can't you see that Sara loves you?"

Nathan met his father's knowing gaze. "She's never said—"

"Never *said?* Actions speak louder than words in my book. She didn't return to Minneapolis for Kyle's sake. If this was all about Kyle, she'd be *here.* I have no doubt about that. She left because she didn't want to hurt your relationship with your son. She didn't want to come between you. She left because you pushed her away. Is that really what you wanted to do?"

When he thought of Sara, Nathan saw her sweet smile, heard her voice, felt her hands on his body. She'd made him feel again, and that feeling had been uncomfortable, risky, unnerving. In a few short weeks she'd turned his life upside down, and he'd fought against that. He'd tried to right it. But what he hadn't realized, until this minute, was that his life wouldn't be right again until she was with him...until she was in his arms.

"By now she probably hates me and resents the distance I've caused between her and Kyle. I know I've hurt her."

"I don't think Sara could hate anyone, least of all you. It seems to me she might even be the forgiving sort...if a man was willing to eat a little humble pie."

"I haven't had much experience at that," Nathan admitted wryly.

"Yeah, I guessed that. But there's a first time for everything."

As hope filled Nathan's heart, a smile crossed his lips. "A first time for everything," he agreed.

Nathan knocked on Sara's office door on December 30, still not knowing what he was going to say. He'd thought about waiting and going to her apartment later so they'd have complete privacy. But he couldn't wait. He wanted her answer *now*.

Her letter to Kyle had been long and funny, filled with everything a little boy would want to hear. She hadn't mentioned whether she was working long hours again…or if she was seeing Ted.

In the course of Nathan's life, he'd always felt confident and sure of the next action he took. Today he didn't, and he guessed that was part of the humble pie his father had spoken of.

Sara's "Come in" was crisp and businesslike.

Taking a deep breath, he pushed open the door and stepped inside.

She was standing at her file cabinet, inserting a folder.

"Sara." Her name came out sounding like a caress. He'd missed her so much, he could hardly resist going to her and taking her into his arms.

She spun around. "Nathan!" She looked stricken, rather than happy to see him.

"I know you're busy, but I need to talk to you." He shut the door, didn't stop at her desk but went around it to where she was standing.

"Is there a problem with Kyle?"

Of course she'd think this was about Kyle.

"Kyle misses you, but that's not why I'm here. I came to talk about *us*."

"Us?"

"If there *is* an us. I know it probably seems to you as if I've done everything I could to push you away."

She glanced down at her hands, but he wouldn't let her evade him. He wanted to see the emotions in those beautiful green eyes.

Lifting her chin, he spoke as honestly as he could. "From the first moment I saw you, I was attracted to you. You turned me on so fast, you took my breath away. The fact I couldn't control the desire I was feeling made me angry. I didn't *want* to feel it. But the more we were together, I realized how good feeling alive could be again. You exasperated me and frustrated me, but you made me laugh, too. And the way you and Kyle connected… The truth is, I wanted you to leave because you were causing upheaval in my ordinary, day-to-day, matter-of-fact life. You see, I had learned how to live with missing Colleen. That state of mind had become comfortable for me."

"Nathan—"

"Listen to me, Sara. This isn't easy for me to say. Missing Colleen wasn't only rooted in love, it was rooted in guilt. I just realized the extent of it a few days ago. I kept pushing for Colleen to get pregnant. I kept pushing for the new procedures. She went along because she loved me. So, when she died in childbirth, I not only experienced grief, but I felt guilt, too. Dad made me see I was holding on to her, not just because of Kyle, but because of that guilt. In a way, I felt as if I'd caused her death. If I'd said, 'We can adopt,' or 'Let's stop and just enjoy being married,' she'd still be alive."

Sara's face was pale, her eyes sad as she concluded, "But you do still love her."

"Some part of me will always love her. But she's a memory now." He took Sara by the shoulders. "*You* are real. *You* are my future. If you can forgive me."

She studied his face. "Are you here because of Kyle? Because if you are—"

He clasped her tighter, filled with the urgency to make her understand. "No, I'm not here because of Kyle. I told you I'm here because of *us*. I love you, Sara. I know you think I took you to bed just because I needed a hot body. That wasn't true. If I gave you that impression, I'm so sorry. After we made love, I didn't know what to think or how to act. Making love with you shook me up more than I could ever admit. Do you want to know why?"

She nodded.

"Because when we made love I felt a soul-deep union with you."

This time he said the words slower and louder, so they'd sink in. "*I love you*. This morning I put away the pictures of Colleen, except for one on the bookshelf and one in Kyle's room. I want pictures of *us* scattered everywhere, the two of us together and the two of us with Kyle. I know your job is here. Your career is here. I don't particularly want to work in finance again, but I'm sure I could find something in Minneapolis that would suit me. Where we live isn't important to me. What's important to me right now is the answer to a question. Will you marry me?"

She looked absolutely stunned.

"Say something," he commanded.

"I...I can't have more children. If that's important to you—"

"*You* are important to me. If we want more children, we can adopt them."

Finally letting herself believe him, maybe finally seeing the love in his eyes, she wrapped her arms around his neck and jubilantly gave him the answer he wanted to hear. "Yes, I'll marry you!"

There were tears in her voice, and when he kissed her, he found the desire, the acceptance and the promise he'd always discovered in their kisses. Now he could give in to that desire freely. He could revel in her acceptance. He could return the promise.

They were breathless when they broke away from each other. He wouldn't let her go far, and he kept his arms around her.

She laughed and stroked his jaw. "You might not care where we live, but *I* do. Being a part of this law firm isn't what I want anymore. I can practice law anywhere. I can open an office in Rapid Creek. I love the lodge and everything about the area. But most of all, I love *you*."

"I was afraid I'd blown whatever we had. When I read your letter, I knew you were the most unselfish woman in the world, leaving the way you did."

"It tore me apart to leave like that. But I couldn't face you, knowing you might be glad I was going."

His arms wrapped her a little tighter. "Promise you'll never leave again."

"I promise I'll spend the rest of my life by your side."

Then Nathan kissed Sara once more, looking forward to a future he hadn't even dreamed of before he met her. Now they would dream together and make those dreams come true.

Epilogue

When Kyle saw Sara, he gave a yelp of surprise and ran to her, hugging her hard. "You came back!"

Nathan stood behind Sara, and she could feel his presence as well as his love. Last night had been a honeymoon experience, although they weren't married yet. They would be soon, though.

Stooping, she took her son into her arms. "I came back."

Nathan hunkered down to Kyle's eye level, too. "I asked Sara to marry me. She's going to live with us always."

"Really? You're *really* going to be my mom?" Kyle waited for her answer with wide-eyed anticipation.

"I'm really going to be your mom."

Galen and Val had been standing in the kitchen. They

came to Sara then, both of them wearing approving expressions.

When Sara straightened, Galen gave her a hug. "When's the big day?"

"As soon as we can arrange it," Nathan declared. Wrapping his arm around Sara's waist, he accepted Val's congratulations. With a grin, he asked, "Can you help us plan a party for next weekend?"

"What kind of party?" Her eyes were dancing at the prospect.

"An engagement party. I want to invite all our friends. Then I can introduce Sara as my wife-to-be…and Kyle's mother."

The idea that Nathan would open up his life again, for her, brought tears to Sara's eyes.

Galen said, "We haven't had a party in a long time. And Val might need some help. We can have that new deli cater it, and Val can supervise. She's good at that."

Val looked surprised at Galen's praise, and blushed. Sara felt vibrations there…as if they'd become genuine friends. Maybe more.

As Sara slipped out of her coat, Kyle asked, "Did Dad tell you I'm gonna go to preschool soon?" He appeared to be excited about the prospect.

After laying her coat over the side of a chair, she took Kyle's hand and led him to the sofa. "Your dad told me last night. How do you feel about that?"

"I can play more. And learn a lot. But…I don't wanna get sick there."

Quickly, Nathan stepped in to reassure their son. "You'll always have your inhaler in your backpack. Mrs. Morton will have one, too. And her house is only a half block from the hospital if you need to go there. Sara and I will check in on you a lot. I think you'll be fine, as fine as you would be here."

Last night, after making love most of the evening, she and Nathan had discussed many topics. Kyle, of course, was the main one. Nathan had told her he'd looked into preschool and was happy with the one he'd found. Sara knew letting go of Kyle even for a few hours a day would be difficult for him. But he was attempting to do what was best for him.

The evening flew by as Sara played with Kyle, made plans with Val and happily let Nathan kiss her whenever they found a few minutes alone. That night, they put Kyle to bed together. After they'd both kissed him good-night, he snuggled into the covers, looking like the happiest little boy on earth.

She knew the feeling.

As soon as they stepped into the living room, Nathan took her into his arms and pressed his lips to hers. Then, smiling, he clasped her hand and tugged her to the sofa.

Pulling a small box from his pocket, he knelt down on one knee before her.

"Nathan?"

He smiled up at her. "I bought this before we left Minneapolis while you were tying up loose ends at your office." He took a ring from the box. It was a diamond, a beautifully set oval in an antique-style setting.

"I love you, Sara. The depth of that love makes me shake my head in wonder. Will you accept this ring and a lifetime with me?"

She realized she had absolutely no doubts when she replied, "I love you, Nathan. I want to spend every day with you for the rest of our lives."

He slipped the ring onto her finger, kissed her palm and gazed up at her with all the feeling her love had set free.

After he rose to his feet, he lifted her into his arms and carried her to their bedroom.

When he closed the door, she knew their happily-ever-after had just begun.

$1.00 OFF

The bestselling Lakeshore Chronicles continue with *Snowfall at Willow Lake*, a story of what comes after a woman survives an unspeakable horror and finds her way home, to healing and redemption and a new chance at happiness.

SUSAN WIGGS

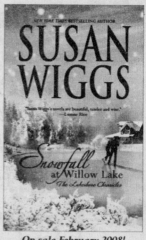

On sale February 2008!

SAVE $1.00 off the purchase price of **SNOWFALL AT WILLOW LAKE** by Susan Wiggs.

Offer valid from February 1, 2008, to April 30, 2008.
Redeemable at participating retail outlets. Limit one coupon per purchase.

52608168

5 65373 00076 2 (8100) 0 11463

Bundles of Joy—
coming next month
to Superromance

Experience the romance, excitement and joy with 6 heartwarming titles.

BABY, I'M YOURS #1476 by *Carrie Weaver*

ANOTHER MAN'S BABY
(The Tulanes of Tennessee)
#1477 by *Kay Stockham*

THE MARINE'S BABY (9 Months Later)
#1478 by *Rogenna Brewer*

BE MY BABIES (Twins)
#1479 by *Kathryn Shay*

THE DIAPER DIARIES (Suddenly a Parent)
#1480 by *Abby Gaines*

HAVING JUSTIN'S BABY (A Little Secret)
#1481 by *Pamela Bauer*

Exciting, Emotional and Unexpected!

*Look for these Superromance titles in March 2008.
Available wherever books are sold.*

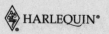

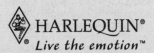

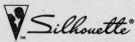

COMING NEXT MONTH

SPECIAL EDITION

#1885 THE SHEIK AND THE PREGNANT BRIDE—Susan Mallery
Desert Rogues
When mechanic Maggie Collins was dispatched to Prince Qadir's desert home to restore his Rolls-Royce, she quickly discovered his love life could use a tune-up, too. Qadir was more than game, but would Maggie's pregnancy shocker stall the prince's engines?

#1886 PAGING DR. DADDY—Teresa Southwick
The Wilder Family
Plastic surgeon to the stars David Wilder, back in Walnut River and the hospital his father once ran, was on a mission of mercy—to perform reconstructive surgery on a little girl badly injured in an auto accident. Would Courtney Albright, the child's resilient, irresistible mother, cause him to give up his L.A. ways for hometown love?

#1887 MOMMY AND THE MILLIONAIRE—Crystal Green
The Suds Club
Unwed and pregnant, Naomi Shannon left her small town for suburban San Francisco, where she made fast friends at the local Laundromat. Sharing her ups and downs and watching the soaps with the Suds Club regulars was a relaxing treat…until gazillionaire David Chandler came along, and Naomi's life took a soap opera turn of its own!

#1888 ROMANCING THE COWBOY—Judy Duarte
The Texas Homecoming
Someone was stealing from Granny, ranch owner Jared Clayton's adoptive mother. So naturally, he gave Granny's new bookkeeper, Sabrina Gonzalez, a real earful. But forget the missing money—a closer accounting of the situation showed that Jared had better watch out before Sabrina stole his heart!

#1889 DAD IN DISGUISE—Kate Little
Baby Daze
When wealthy architect Jack Sawyer tried to cancel a sperm donation, he discovered his baby had already been born to single mother Rachel Reilly. So Jack went undercover as a handyman at her house to spy. Jack fell for the boy...and for Rachel—hard. But when the dad took off his disguise, all hell broke loose....

#1890 HIS MIRACLE BABY—Karen Sandler
To honor his deceased wife's wishes, sporting goods mogul Logan Rafferty needed a surrogate mother for their embryos. Her confidante Shani Jacoby would be perfect—but she was his sworn enemy. Still loyal to her best friend, though, Shani chose to carry Logan's miracle baby—and soon an even bigger miracle—of love—was on their horizon.

SSECNM0208